Passport to Perdita

A novelette

S.B. Borgersen

PASSPORT FOR PERDITA

Attention schools and businesses: for discounted copies on large orders, please contact the publisher directly.

For information contact:
Unsolicited Press
Portland, Oregon
www.unsolicitedpress.com
orders@unsolicitedpress.com
619-354-8005

Cover Design: Kathryn Gerhardt
Editor: S. Stewart
ISBN: 978-1-963115-13

For Tilly

Author's Note

This story was drafted over Thanksgiving weekend, for a 3-day novel project, some years ago. Inspiration came from two intriguing old passports discovered in a pop-up antique store. But that's another story…

May 2023

'If you look for truth, you may find comfort in the end.'

C.S. Lewis

'The other side of life? It is true all life has another side, and we will only find it if we look.'

Perdita Drummond

Passport to Perdita

1.

Gordon Drummond buried his father three days ago. He remembers nothing of the funeral except how cold and empty he felt in the family pew at the front of the church. How stinging freezing the cemetery was and that his nose just wouldn't stop running. He had no handkerchief in the pocket of his borrowed dark grey overcoat, but he'd had the foresight to grab a piece of paper towel from the kitchen before leaving for the church. The rough dollar store paper towel made his nose red and sore.

It is still sore now as he sits on the sofa pondering where his life will go from this point. He pokes the wood stove with the brass poker, using the stabbing action his mother taught him years before, and sits back watching the flames come to life through the glass-fronted door. He swallows hard. "It's going to be okay, Pea," he says to his dog.

The ageing white whippet jumps onto the sofa and curls herself on Gordon's lap, arches her neck until her nose is firmly tucked under her hind leg and closes her eyes. Gordon scratches behind her folded ears, "Goodnight, Pea," he says. "Just us now, old girl."

Gordon watches—without really seeing—the solitary black flea speed through the fine white hairs of the whippet. He is thinking back to the funeral. He can still feel hands gently patting his shoulder afterwards. Faces melded, one with the other. The words, 'Sorry for your loss,' mouthed in lipsticked 'O's wriggle though his mind like the elusive flea running to the dog's groin. One by one the faces begin to come back to him. Some are old friends of his dad's. And some are complete strangers. Not people from around here at all. He watches the black flea as it emerges briefly before burrowing back through the fine white hairs of Pea's coat. What Gordon sees, as he watches the flea, is clear now—a dark figure of a woman stepping carefully through the snowy pathways of the cemetery. Dressed all in black, she has long, dark mahogany hair and no hat. She speaks to no one and is gone before he catches even a glimpse of her face.

He cannot bring himself to go to bed. The fire has a rosy glow, and with Pea now curled behind his legs, he undoes the waistband of his jeans, pulls the plaid wool blanket over his shoulders and lays back, staring at the ceiling.

It is quiet without Dad, he thinks. The old man would normally be making that late night cup of tea about now. Reading through the local weekly newspaper, again, looking through the obituaries for names of old friends; people he went to school with, checking out the deals in the flyers, muttering through his cigarette about the price of steak and toilet paper. All before Pea's final nightly walk around the loop.

Gordon supposes that the dog was always really his father's dog, even though she was not intended to be. She came as an eight-week-old puppy from Ontario. All bones and beseeching seal-like eyes. "My, but you're so perdy," said Andrew Ainslie Drummond, dipping his little finger into his milky tea and letting the puppy suckle. That was the beginning of the bond between the two.

Gordon was an only child. His father travelled with his work as a cable mechanism specialist. His mother, Maryanne, was somewhat of a single parent because of her husband's long absences in South America. Gordon was her constant companion from an early age. He didn't know people talked—speculated about their situation—he was too young then.

"Why don't you divorce the bastard?" said her friend Ivy. More than once.

"You could find yourself another man, a good man, take care of you and the boy," said Ivy's friend Ruby.

But Gordon's mother, Maryanne, shook her head every time, saying nothing. She was a good mother, and Andrew always made sure the finances were in order. Ensuring Gordon always had good clothes for school and a new pair of shoes each September.

As the years passed, even though he was a good student, Gordon relinquished the idea of college, preferring to stay close to home, near his mother. He found that figure work and accounting were his strengths and a job in payroll at the mill suited him just fine.

Gordon and his mother were inseparable.

"Unhealthy," said wise Ivy, "for a grown man to spend so much time with his mother." Ivy didn't have the full picture. No-one did.

When Gordon came home from work, Maryanne had his supper ready on the table.

Usually, seafood chowder is made using scallops and haddock and sometimes lobster from the wharf. Or a lamb stew, sometimes a roast with beef, all the meat from the farm on the hill. With Blueberry Grunt or Upside-Down Pineapple Pudding for dessert, recipes from Maryanne's mother's old recipe book with its falling-out pages and handwritten notes in the margins. When he was a little boy, Gordon leafed through the recipe books, admiring the line drawings, reading the ingredients slowly, "What's 'lb'," he said, "and 'oz'?"

"They are pounds and ounces," she said gently, "that's how people weighed the things for the cakes and bread before cups and spoons." She showed him the old scales and he played for hours with the little brass weights and the larger heavier ones, once dropping one on his big toe which swelled up causing all kinds of panic for a few days.

At eight years old he thought that pounds and ounces were much more complicated than cups and spoons but painstakingly wrote a conversion chart for his mother, showing her how many ounces of flour equalled a cup. Maryanne taped it inside the kitchen cupboard door, the cupboard where she kept her rolling pin and mixing bowls. The two spent evenings and weekends together. In winter they sat by the fire discussing planting plans for the spring garden, radishes and heirloom tomatoes, maybe. Zucchini and spinach. And sunflowers, Maryanne always planted some sunflower seeds. She liked the seeds for the winter bird feeders. Finches were her special delight. In the summer, mother and son went fishing at the lake, or weeded the vegetable patch, finishing as the sun dipped down by walking a dog. Not Pea, this was before Pea came along. But there was always a dog with Gordon and Maryanne.

Maryanne died twenty years ago, after seven months of battling pancreatic cancer.

Andrew returned home from South America when the

illness began. He never left her side in all those seven months. This meant Gordon began living with his father in what was, to begin with, an uncomfortable situation. But slowly as the months and then years passed, they fell into a balletic rhythm. Moving around the kitchen preparing individual breakfasts. Reaching for a knife or a plate. Not touching, knowing who would go to the left, or to the right. They sat opposite each other at the kitchen table, Andrew with his weekly newspaper. Gordon staring through the window, down across the bay, to the town on the other side.

His father applied for his old age pension and stayed. Gordon worked to keep them both going, and his father took care of the home and had a hot supper ready when Gordon arrived home each evening at 5.30. Andrew cooked fancy suppers he'd learned to make on his travels through South America. Dishes involving eggplant and fennel. Desserts using mangoes and fruits never heard of before in this part of rural Nova Scotia.

On his way home from the office, Gordon wondered, with pleasant anticipation, just what concoctions his father might have prepared. It was an arrangement that worked. They got to know each other. In a quiet, non-conversational way. Went fishing together on the lake. Kept up Maryanne's garden. Always planting sunflowers ready for the winter and the bird feeders.

Without knowing it, Gordon gave Andrew a taste of Maryanne's life. Many evenings they sat on the deck, watching the sun go down.

"Was she happy?" said Andrew looking into the distance.

"I guess," was Gordon's reply, "but define happy."

"Did she cry for me?"

Gordon was shocked at the question, "If she did, she hid that from me, Dad," he said. "She was strong and very brave, there were times we had nothing. But we made the best of what we had."

Andrew said nothing, staring into the distance. A tear rolled down his cheek. "What?" said Gordon. "Did you want her to spend the years mourning for you?" He knew the words were harsh the second he spat them out, but still felt some things needed saying. "You left us, you know that," he said in a gentler tone.

"I'm sorry, Son."

"It's a bit late for that," said Gordon, offering his father a cold bottle of beer, "but we can't turn the clock back, can we? We must make the best of things, when you're ready, I'll show you some of the things she did with her life."

Andrew's death was unexpected. He was fit and healthy for someone in their eighties and always joked with his doctor who said, 'You're in good shape for your age.' When Gordon got home from work to find Andrew flat on his back on the kitchen floor, the phone still in his hand, he was in disbelief. But he knew, when he looked down at Andrew, he knew that it was all over, that the body lying on the floor was not his dad anymore, that the spirit had gone, and it was just his cold body. Gordon had heard people talk about this at work, how people's features change once their heart stops beating. How they take on a false waxen look. And that is what Gordon remembers now. More than anything. More than the twenty years of living side by side, of the fishing trips, and the exotic suppers. Even the funeral. He wants to remember that if he can, but it just won't come.

As Gordon sinks back on the sofa with Pea, he looks up at the ceiling and sees the indelible image of his father, lying just as he did on the kitchen floor. Waxen and yellow. Gordon sobs.

2.

"Come with us Gordie, come with us, you'll love it." Joslyn Wentzell from work is on the phone. "I don't think," says Gordon. "What about Pea-pod?"

"You can bring her," says Joslyn, "it's a picnic. You can bring your dog and your cooler, it's always loads of fun."

"I'll think about it," says Gordon. He puts the phone down but rests his hand on the receiver. He is having trouble with this new-found social life people are foisting upon him. He supposes it is kindness but doesn't react well to charity. He feels torn. Should he go? The Dog Days Picnic sounds like a casual event. Something where you can just sit around on the lawn with your dog and let them all sniff each other. He can't imagine Joslyn has an ulterior motive. Gordon is in his sixties and with no history of a female partnership. Maybe he seems like a dream come true for someone like Joslyn. "No," Gordon shakes his head and mutters, "I have no time for such nonsense."

In true Nova Scotia style, Gordon is late for his appointment at the lawyer's office. Reg Conrad welcomes him with a handshake and, "Coffee?"

"Okay," says Gordon, "I came out in a rush, didn't get chance..." "Cream and...?"

"Yup, that's good," says Gordon.

Reg Conrad went to The Bay Elementary School with Gordon. They were both 'bookish', the term used in those days for someone who was geeky or nerdish. They spent recesses together, sitting on a flat rock in the corner of the schoolyard sharing each other's discoveries of something scientific, or a hero comic book.

"How's it going, Gordie?" "Ya know. Okay I guess."

"Bet it's quiet in your neck of the woods."

"Too quiet, can't hear myself think sometimes," says Gordon. "Where did life go, Reg?" Reg looks across the desk at his old school friend slumped in the worn leather visitors' chair. Stubble on his chin. Balding head that once was so thick in blond curls. A paunch of a belly beginning to project through the green plaid shirt. He knows Gordon hasn't eaten properly since Andrew died, and it shows.

"Good question," he says, "I often ask myself too. Especially when I look in the mirror in a morning." He pauses. Closes the files on his desk. "Tell you what, Gordie, why don't we leave this paperwork for now and go down the coast for a drive, maybe take in some lunch. I know a great place."

"Don't you have other appointments?" says Gordon.

"I'll get 'em cancelled," says Reg. "There's nothing urgent, all routine stuff." They walk into the outer office, side by side, same step, just as they did as nine-year-olds.

"Louise, can you cancel the rest of today for me?" says Reg. The secretary looks up, surprised. "Just say something urgent has cropped up—you'll handle it," says Reg with a smile. "We'll take my car shall we?" Still smiling, he says to Gordon. "You might like it; it's a hybrid."

The drive along Highway 103 to Lower West Pubnico takes just over two hours of very little traffic. The plow has been through, and high banks of dirty snow thrown up against the pines and spruce bordering the highway make Gordon think of distant lands, of the postcards his father sent each month from the Andes, from Chile, from Panama, and from Venezuela. He closes his eyes. Willie Nelson is singing, 'On the Road Again,' from the quadraphonic music system in Reg's Lexus ...*Goin' places that I've never been. Seein' things that I may never see again...* Gordon can't help but wonder about the life his father had, the life he, Gordon, was not a part of except for the regular postcards and his mother's monthly cheque arriving in an airmail envelope. He wondered why Andrew never talked to him about it in the twenty years they'd finally had together. And sometimes he regrets he never asked.

"What's that?" says Reg. "What?"

"You asked me something," says Reg.

"Oh. Oh no, I was probably dreaming," says Gordon. "Just wondering, that's all.

Wondering what Dad's life was like all those years he was away. Wondering why he never talked about it."

"Did you never go visit him?" says Reg.

"Never invited." says Gordon as they turn off the highway at trunk road 335. The white houses and over-powering churches of the Acadian communities seem like a foreign land to Gordon.

"Never been down here, Gordie?" says Reg. "I'm ashamed to say, I haven't."

"Not even to gawk at the wind farm?" "Nope."

"We'll put that right before we do anything else," says Reg, "it's only 12.30, we've loads of time to eat."

They drive to the end of the point and park the Lexus. The seventeen turbines tower above them. "They say here they are seventy-eight metres tall," says Reg looking up from the information board.

"Do you feel weird?" says Gordon, "do you think they give off some sort of vibe?" "The locals don't like them," says Reg. "They can hear them all the time. Apparently, there are some cases of stress."

"Progress, I suppose," says Gordon climbing back into the car. "Your dad knew about such stuff, didn't he?" says Reg.

"He never said," says Gordon, "I always thought his work was to do with cables under water. At least that's what Ma always said."

The restaurant parking lot has five other cars. "Not busy, still I suppose a Tuesday in the middle of winter is not the most popular time for eating out."

But inside, the place is packed with local lobster fishermen. "Good sign," says Gordon. Reg nods and steers Gordon to a quiet table in the corner. "They do a real good chowder," says Reg. "The liver dinner is good too."

When the server comes over with menus, Reg tells her, "We've already decided. It's the chowder, the liver dinner and two beers. Keith's. Thanks, Kelly."

"You've been here before then," says Gordon.

"Oh yes," says Reg, "it's good to get away from the bay. For some reason people want to share all their legal questions with you over the dinner or supper table. I don't get a break."

"And you're too mild-mannered to tell them?" says

Gordon. "You don't change, do you, Reg." It wasn't a question.

"But today I'm going to make an exception, for you, I thought we needed a change of scenery, and we can still talk about, well, what we need to talk about. Plus, you do look hungry, Gord."

Gordon says nothing. He hates to admit he's not taking care of himself. It is ten days since the funeral, and he can't remember if he's cooked or done any laundry. At least he had a shower before the appointment at Reg's office, but he knows now that he forgot to shave and that his shirt is wrinkled from not being ironed. "Sorry," he says, "I don't know where my mind is right now."

"It's natural," says Reg. "I've seen folks like this so many times before, well in my job I would. But Gordie, you've got no one to share this with. We've got quite a lot of paperwork to get through, and I have some stuff for you that your dad left with me."

Gordon raises his grey eyebrows, says nothing, crumbling the freshly baked tea biscuit on his side plate. He rubs the crumbs back and forth between his thumb and forefinger until there is nothing left on the plate but a sandy pile. He wipes his hands on the table napkin. "Sorry," he says, "this is happening a lot right now."

"Do you think a vacation might help?" says Reg.

"Ha!" Gordon attempts a laugh. "You've got to be kidding. I don't think I've ever been anywhere away from here in my life, unless you count that time we went with the Scouts to PEI."

"Then maybe it's time, Gordie. Maybe it's time to live a

little."

The two men, old school friends, eat their meal without saying too much. They sip their cold beer and look out across the road to the busy wharf, the lobster boats and the large trucks rumbling in from the buyers. Gordon begins to realise it was a good idea to get away from familiar surroundings. But he has no idea that Reg wants him with open eyes and mind for what he has in store when they get back to the office.

3.

"I'm going to tell you a story," says Joslyn. She has come round to Gordon's after work with a pie. They sit in the kitchen; the wood stove is doing a good job. Pea is curled up on an old quilt in front of the fire with Louie, Joslyn's retired greyhound. The two dogs look alike. Both white with black dots here and there. "Like a matching pair," Joslyn says.

Gordon doesn't want to make too much of that. He likes Joslyn as a work colleague, but he doesn't want to think of matching pairs. Not right now in any case. He has too many other things on his mind.

"I do appreciate you coming round," he says, "and the pie is excellent—you remembered how much I love pumpkin."

"Not just a pretty face," she replies with a grin, crinkling up her nose, exaggerating the wrinkles around her eyes. "I thought you might be hungry for some home cooking; it was never really your thing, was it?"

Gordon laughs; a dry laugh. But it's a laugh; something he hasn't done in a while. He feels a slight ease in his tension. "No, but you know that. Mom was the cook until she died, then Dad took over. Pathetic isn't it, for someone my age? I don't really know how to look after myself. But I'm learning," he adds, too quickly, wanting to preempt any suggestion on Joslyn's part.

She laughs again, "Don't worry," she says. "Not trying to muscle in, I've seen too many others make that mistake."

Gordon hasn't a clue what she's talking about, but delves into his pie, hoping the cinnamon doesn't cause the heartburn he had the last time. "You said you were going to tell me a story," he says through a mouthful of pie.

"Oh yes, you didn't come with us to the Dog Days picnic, I know. My goodness, you missed a good day."

Gordon gets up to put the coffee pot on the stove and settles back down to listen.

Joslyn continues, "There's a young girl volunteer at the kennels. She is always there when a new load of greyhounds come up from the track in Florida. She helps out with cleaning the kennels, walking the dogs, bathing them, talking to them, soothing them. She just loves them to bits."

"How old?" says Gordon.

"What, the dogs? Oh, you mean the girl. I guess she's about eighteen I suppose." "Jos?"

"Yup."

"Would you mind if you don't tell me now. I'm guessing this is a lovely sad and happy story. I'd just rather you keep it for another time. Sorry."

"Jeez, Gord, no, I'm sorry, I keep forgetting all you've been through. I was going to tell you how she'd been through a bad patch and working with the dogs has helped her turn her life around. Don't take any notice of my babble. But seriously, is there anything else I can do to help?"

"Well, it's funny you should ask..." "Yeah?"

"Two things, and I should have told you this before you came over. It's just that I keep forgetting..."

"Yes?"

"Well, I think Pea has a flea or two."

"Oh Lordie Gordie, that ain't nothing," says Joslyn, "I'll take care of that for you. Let me take her home with me for half an hour. Bring her back all right as rain, how about that?"

"That would be great, such a relief. I noticed right after the funeral, but I had so much on my mind."

"It's funny that there're fleas about right now, but I hear a lot of people saying. So what was the other thing?"

"Other?" says Gordon.

"Yes, you said there were two things."

"I don't know how to put this Jos, but I may need to go away for a time. Maybe a couple of months, there's something I have to do for Dad. I just wonder if Pea-pod could come and stay with you and Louie."

4.

Gordon had never before opened the large oak desk in the parlour. It sits, where it always has, on the opposite wall to the bay window. It is a large drop-fronted desk with ornate barley-twist scrolls along each side. First, his mother took care of it. Polishing it each week with lavender polish. Dusting it each Wednesday. Keeping all the bills in one pigeonhole, and the receipts in another. Personal addresses in one section. Stamps and envelopes in another. The big drawer, also locked, was where folders with insurance policies, birth certificates and other such documents were kept. Such things had always been a mystery to Gordon. His mother never taught him that side of life; she took care of those things for him.

When his father eventually returned home, he took care of the desk, keeping the keys on his keychain in his pocket.

Gordon thinks now that was irresponsible of them. He had no idea there was so much to running a home. Things like property tax and stuff like that. He was just thankful there was no mortgage. The property had belonged to his grandparents, who inherited it through the family. The house, always known as The Drummond, stood back from the road, slightly elevated above its neighbours, looking down to its own waterfront, its dock, and across the bay to town. After the legal talks with Reg, Gordon knew the house and land were now all his. And he knew the value. Such properties were changing hands for more than a million dollars right now. It certainly gave him reason to think and think hard. Especially after Reg mentioned maybe Gordie should start to 'live a little.' That was the way Gordon remembered Reg putting it, again, during the second trip down the coast for a discussion over lunch.

"Life's too short, you know," said Reg. "Take a trip down to South America; see what your old man was really up to."

Gordie had laughed then, "I don't even have a passport," he said, "never had one, never needed one."

But the seed of the idea began to take root.

He sits at the desk and turns the key in the top lock and gently lowers the heavy lid to rest on the pulled-out barley scroll arms. The contents are impossibly tidy. He wants to take time going through everything and begins with the top pigeonhole on the right. The bills. There is just one. An invoice for FedEx. It is in the name of Mr. A.A. Drummond. All it states is, *for courier services to Chile $59.95.*

Gordon scratches the side of his nose. It is twenty years since his father was in Chile. Why would he be sending something by courier only a few days before his death? There is nothing to connect the bill with anything, so Gordon continues to the next pigeonhole. The receipts. They consist of mostly slips for gas and groceries. Gordon isn't sure why such receipts would need keeping. He isn't sure if they could be used for income tax. He fingers the curling corners of the tiny scraps of paper, mostly cash register stubs. Well-thumbed. Checked over more than once. Stapled by each month. Organised. Everything accounted for. One bundle, folded, right at the bottom of the heap, is from FedEx. For courier services to Chile. Ten years' worth. Mostly for around $20 each time. Gordon takes a deep breath and wonders just what business his father was conducting in Chile right until he died.

He calls Reg. "I've no idea," says Reg, "he was pretty vague with me, just wanted you to have the keys to the desk so that you would have everything to go through at your leisure. If you want me to come over and help, any time, Gord, you just have to say."

"It's okay for now," says Gordon, "It just bothers me seeing all these courier documents. He must've been sending something when I was at work because I have no recollection of FedEx calling at the house at all. Ever. I wonder why he never said anything."

"Have you thought anymore about going to find out in person?" says Reg. "Again, if you want company, I might be able to help."

"You're a good friend, Reg. I'll give it more thought. I may well take you up on that offer." Gordon replaces the old telephone receiver. He can't bring himself to go any further through the desk, but knows it will have to be done, so he unlocks the drawer and takes out the file folders, bringing them over to the coffee table. He makes himself a sandwich with his favourite local bacon and sits back with Pea at his side.

"Now then, old girl, let's take a look through these, see if they can shed any light," he says.

Daylight fades into wintery dusk before Gordon has made any headway with the files. He gets up, stretches, closes the curtains, throws another log on the fire. "I suppose you need to go out," he says to the dog, who looks up at him with her melting eyes as if to say, 'thank you for reading my mind.'

Pea uncoils herself from the sofa, two front legs on the rug first and then allows the back ones to drop down after her. Gordon puts on her red fleece coat for her, then his own thick plaid jacket before making their way down the driveway to the ice-covered dock.

The moon is high over the frozen bay, but still, it reflects on the blue-white expanse. The silence is overwhelming, and Gordon reminds himself how lucky he is to live in such a serene part of the world. He sees recent fox tracks, finding some reassurance that wildlife is still wild and kicking. He knows how cold it must be for them, but up in the woods behind the house there is plenty of shelter, cavernous hollows beneath tree roots and granite boulders. He knows the property like he knows his own face. He is pretty sure he is blessed.

But still there is the loneliness. The fear that he has no family left now. If only he'd had brothers or sisters. Even cousins, that would have been something. But there is no-one. Just him and Pea and a couple of colleagues who want to be friends. And his old school friend Reg. His lawyer.

Gordon tries imagining what his life will be like now. An empty house to come home to. Learning how to cook, clean and do his own laundry. Maybe he should go looking for a wife, or at least a companion. All these questions. And no answers popping out of the woodwork. Still, for some reason Reg thinks Gordon's father has left all possible answers in the large oak desk and maybe, just maybe, he should stick at it tonight.

"Come on then, old girl," he says to the whippet, "let's get back inside where it's warm."

She looks up at him as if she understands, and together they walk back up to the house and in through the back door to the kitchen.

5.

Joslyn shows Gordon how to do online research. He uses a computer at work but has never had the desire to have one at home. "Google is your friend," she says, getting as close to Gordon as she can, showing him how to search for keywords on the new laptop he's bought in town. "What are you looking for exactly?" She leans across, letting her breast catch his shoulder.

But Gordon is reticent. Either to respond to her advances or to share any concerns he has about his father's activities with anyone other than Reg. "Just stuff," he says. "Things about other countries; I'm thinking of travelling a bit as you know, that's why I asked if you could take care of her for me." He reaches down under the dining table where Pea is curled against his legs.

"But if you tell me more, I can help," she says.

"It's okay, Jos, honestly, I'm just doodling around for something to do, idle curiosity you might call it."

So they leave it at that and open a couple of beers, watching the afternoon sun dip down over the horizon. "You won't find what you're looking for out over there," she says, grinning.

He looks up, he knows her well enough to be honest, "I know," he says, "I'm just regretting not doing more with my life, that's all."

"Don't have regrets," she says, "you're a good man, Gordon Drummond. You don't have to be a jet-setting

32

millionaire to be a good man."

Gordon is glad Joslyn doesn't know the whole story, not that he knows all of it himself. But the more he finds out, the more he realises he will never need to worry about money again.

Loneliness maybe, but not money. Then he reminds himself of the one thing his mother often said, that money doesn't buy happiness, bringing his thoughts right back to where he started.

After Joslyn leaves in her rattling Toyota pickup, he goes back to the laptop and searches the cost of flights to Valparaiso, Chile, the one place that seems a constant in all the papers of his father. He is pleasantly surprised to find that $1500 will buy a return ticket from Halifax to Santiago, but not to Valparaiso. He would want to stopover there for a week or so to check out some Chilean bonds he'd found in a yellow wax paper envelope in the desk drawer. He looks at the calendar and thinks mid-February to mid-April would be the best time. That would give him the opportunity to get more information together and make arrangements. The biggest one being to apply for early retirement.

Having thought all this through, Gordon feels a quickening in his stomach, an excitement never felt before as he contemplates a real life-changer. He picks up the eight-page passport application Reg dropped off yesterday and begins to fill out the details.

He feels just like he did when he went away with the Scouts to The Island. He was thirteen and his mother bought him new underwear and socks and some play clothes from Bob's Store in town. She washed and ironed and folded them all and packed them in a small cardboard suitcase for him, attaching a luggage label stating that 'this case belongs to Gordon Andrew Drummond, Indian Point, Lunenburg County. If found, please return.' Gordon kept the label in a box of small treasures in his bedroom with his scout badges and some black marbles. He wonders, only fleetingly, if the label would do to attach to his suitcase for his trip to South America. Which brings him to thinking about suitcases.

He doesn't really want to splash out on a new one. His father's travel equipment is all in the bedroom that was first his parents', then his mother's and then, finally, his father's. He climbs the stairs, stepping gently on the sixth tread, which always creaks, and opens the door to the room he has probably only ever been in half a dozen times. It is dark, with the royal blue flowered curtains closed. The large bed is cloaked in a matching royal blue satin bedspread. The head of the bed is high, dark mahogany and finely carved with angels and exotic fruit. Gordon had never studied the detail of the bed head before. He runs his hands across the highly polished top, still wondering at the strange relationship that was his parents' marriage.

On top of the matching armoire is a set of three old suitcases; stacked on top of each other. Gordon stands on a chair and lifts down the top one. It is in a faded green canvas and has leather corners with studs. It is heavier than he thought it would be, but the second is even heavier. When it comes to the third, the biggest, Gordon finds he needs all his strength to lift the case down.

He places each one on the over-sized bed and tries to open them. They are locked. Just like he knew they would be. Every possible key from the desk and also the package Reg handed to him are in his pocket. Gordon has got accustomed to finding things locked and learned quickly that there is no need to be running back and forth trying keys. Old suitcase keys are easy to recognise. "They don't make them like this anymore," he mutters, turning the key in the lock of the smallest case.

Gordon is not ready for the contents. There are two purple velvet drawstring bags about six inches square with hand embroidered monograms—'D'—in yellow gold silk. He takes a deep breath and pulls out small trinkets, lockets mostly, on gold chains. There are five in total. He holds his breath and carefully pulls back the catch on the first. There is a photograph of a young girl. And a lock of dark brown hair.

Gordon lays back on the bed with a pillow propped up against the carved headboard. He angles the shade of the bedside light to give him a better view of the photograph in the locket. He guesses the girl to be about five or six years old, and that the lock of hair would be from her first haircut, maybe to start school. He doesn't recognise the face. He knows his father's sister was fair and died of lung problems when she was only two years old. Gordon has no idea who this might be. Only one locket has a curl of hair, the others have photographs of adults, again no-one he recognises. He carefully replaces them in the velvet pouch and opens the other. This one contains an identity card in a foreign language. Bound in red leather with gold lettering, his father's name, A. Drummond, and the name of a company. Gordon assumes the firm he worked for. He has no idea why his father would keep it in a velvet pouch in a locked suitcase.

He leaves the suitcase open on the bed and goes downstairs, taking the ID card with him.

Turning on the laptop, he begins some research into the company name. And variations of the name. Gordon is shocked that results quickly list down the screen for Perdita Drummond Gold. It is a mining company. There is a quote from The Financial Post regarding a court case against the mine and unresolved disputes over its impact on the environment.

Gordon shivers. He knows now that he has cracked open the lid on a world totally unknown to him and he has no idea what to do about it. He looks at the old Gebrueder clock on the mantel. It is twenty minutes to ten. Gordon picks up the phone and dials Reg's number.

6.

"This scares me shitless," Gordon says to Reg.

"Slow down, slow down," says Reg, "start again, what in the be-Jesus have you found?" "I opened a suitcase," says Gordon, "found an ID card."

"Yes, yes?"

"I looked it up on the computer," says Gordon, feeling a tad braver than ten minutes ago, "and found it's an ID card for a gold mine in Chile."

"Holy suff'rin'," says Reg. "I had no idea. Do you want me to come over?"

"It's late," says Gordon, "I know, but I'll never sleep with all this lot laid out in front of me. And there's more."

"More?"

"Yes, there's a locket and some hair. No one I recognise."

"I've a bottle of Scotch, not yet opened. Stay right where you are, Gordie, I'll be right over."

Gordon puts down the phone and says, "Do you need to get out, stretch your legs, old girl?" to Pea. "If so, we'd better git 'er done before Reg gets here, we may be at this all night."

They are still out on the dock when Reg's Lexus pulls up and the three walk into the house together. The kitchen has a warmth only a wood stove can give; slightly smoky, comforting. Reg takes off his snow covered boots and pulls a pair of carpet slippers out of his coat pocket. "Thought these would be a good idea," he says, "I suspect we are in for a long night."

Gordon pads around the kitchen in his sock feet. Thick fishermen's socks that keep the cold out. The two men sit at the kitchen table with Pea at their feet on a blanket. Gordon fetches two tumblers and Reg opens the Scotch.

"It's been a long time since I've done anything like this," says Reg. Gordon raises an eyebrow. "So, it's happened before?"

"No. God no. Nothing like this," says Reg. "But there have been times when clients have gone through a rough patch, and I've helped them sort things out. It usually happens at night."

"Is that how you see me. And this?" says Gordon.

"No, Gordie. This is different. Very different. Let's get a drink in us and then we can make a start."

By 3 am. the two have emptied all three suitcases. The contents tell quite the story. There are many photographs of people Gordon doesn't know. Except those of his father, wearing shorts, standing under tropical trees. Smiling a smile Gordon has never seen before. And with other people, sitting outside bars, around tables. Bottles with foreign labels strewn around. Photos taken in nightclubs. On riverbanks. And in mountains.

The other people include a tall woman with long, dark, flowing hair. Two small children in shifts. Gordon assumes they are girls from the hair styles too. He wonders who the lock of hair in the locket belongs to.

"Reg, what do you reckon at the pictures?" says Gordon.

"Hard to say," says Reg, "but at first glance, I'd say your

father had another family."

Gordon says nothing. Reg has confirmed what he already feels. A mix of shock and excitement. Excitement at the possibility that he isn't alone in the world after all. That he does have family somewhere.

And that somewhere looks like it's in Chile. South America. But his feeling is mixed with a tinge of sadness. To think that all those years, when his father was away, he was with another family. Coming home from work in the evenings to sit down with them and have supper. To go out at weekends on trips to rivers, and mountains, and stand under exotic trees. And then in the evenings, to sit in nightclubs with another woman. Another wife? Wearing clothes never to be seen in these here parts. While Gordon's mother, Andrew's REAL wife, scrimped and saved to make ends meet. Who never had a social life of her own, never cavorted with another man. Who dedicated her life to Gordon.

"I need another drink," says Gordon. Together the two men sit back at the table, glasses in hand and look at each other.

"You, well we I suppose, have taken the lid off a crock of worms by the looks of things," says Reg. "Sometimes I wish people would sort out their messes before they shuffle off to the graveyard, and not leave this trail of unanswered questions for those left behind."

There is a silence that carries their thoughts around the kitchen, over their heads, swirling around the old wooden shelves with their dishes and pots. In and out of the pantry with its stock of canned tomatoes and peaches and beans until those thoughts disappear and reappear as words again.

"The thing is Reg..." "Hmmm."

"The things is… what do I do about it?"

"We," says Reg. "We. If you would like, I'll help you with this. WE can find out as much as we can without alerting anyone. That means not hurting anyone either. So far, you are the only person who knows something of both sides of the story, well I guess so. Or would your father have been open with these other people?" He waves his hands across the piles of photos. "Open about the fact that he had a family back here in Canada?"

"Don't know," says Gordon, "but you know there were strangers at the funeral. There was a woman…"

"I remember," says Reg. "I stood near the back you know. I don't know if you realised I was there, but I did come, for you as much as anyone. I did see a strange face or two. Not folks from around here. But your dad did travel a lot years ago. And he did come to see me, first when he came back, to sort out your mother's estate, and then off and on, to ask me to handle his own affairs."

Gordon looks up at Reg. "Thanks," he says. "What for?"

"Just thanks, I reckon we should sleep on this and look at it with fresh eyes in the morning."

"You're right," says Reg, "I can't drive you know, not after all this whisky. Can I have the sofa?'

"Sure," says Gordon, "I'll fetch pillows and blankets. You know you'll have Pea for company."

"Lovely," says Reg.

Gordon tosses and turns all night. Whether it is because someone else is in the house, or because images of foreign women and palm trees keep floating through his mind, he doesn't know. By 5 a.m., he knows it's no good and goes down to the kitchen to make coffee. What he sees is evidence that Reg couldn't sleep either. The table has neat piles of photographs, all categorised and dated with sticky notes on top. Stacks of papers again with yellow sticky notes—three piles saying *Chile, New York, Panama.* And on top of everything is a passport. It is an old passport with the corner clipped and 'cancelled' stamped across the name: Mr. Andrew Ainslie Drummond.

Gordon puts down the coffeepot and looks for Reg. No sign of Reg or Pea, so he knows they're out for a walk. There has been a fine falling of snow through the night. Reg's car is covered, as is the front lawn rolling down to the dock. Two sets of prints trail through the snow. Reg's boots and Pea's fine little paw prints. Heading in the direction of the estuary. Gordon knows it will not be long before Pea's feet are too cold to withstand the snow and they'll be back wanting to be warmed. He starts a pot of oatmeal alongside the coffee, picks up the passport and sits in his father's armchair by the stove.

42

7.

"What do you think?" says Reg, coming through the entryway, shaking off the snow. "Shocked," says Gordon. "But there had to be something, didn't there? He couldn't have just lived down there all those years, just to work and send money back. I wonder if Mom knew." "I think she might've," says Reg. "That's the sad part. In addition, it seems he might have more assets than's in his will here. You'd better sit down."

"Let me feed Pea her breakfast first," says Gordon, "then you can show me what you've come up with. Coffee?"

"Can I?" Reg indicates the laptop.

"Sure," says Gordon, ladling out a couple of spoonfuls of oatmeal for Pea, putting it by the window to cool.

"While you were sleeping, I found a law office in Santiago, Chile. I reckon if we speak with them, they may shed some light," says Reg, turning the laptop around for Gordon to see the website. "There may have been a second will, dealing with all of his assets down there."

"Is that allowed?" says Gordon.

"I think so, especially if he had residence there, and all things were kept absolutely separate, as we see they are. And you may or may not like this idea, but I think we should do it face to face. One-on-one, if you like."

Gordon stops between the stove and the table, coffeepot in hand, "You mean go down there?"

"Yes."

"I'd already decided I should," says Gordon, "although, as you know, I haven't a clue how to go about it. I did send off for my passport though."

"That's good," says Reg, "I did wonder. I think it best if we both go, like I suggested earlier."

They book flights with Air Canada online. Reg uses his loyalty card for upgrades and the dates are pretty much what Gordon suggested. February to April. Reg assures Gordon that taking time off is no problem for him; he has new partners hired and has been looking for a way to step back a little, take some time for himself.

"This'll be a trip of a lifetime for me," says Reg.

"Me too," says Gordon. "I've already made arrangements for Pea to stay with Jos. It was a bit difficult; I reckon Jos fancies me, and wanted to tag along." The two men laugh. Good belly laughs. Something Gordon hasn't done for weeks.

"It's Christmas next week," says Reg. "What do you fancy doing?"

"Me?" says Gordon. "Haven't even thought about it, haven't you got family and stuff?' "No-one," says Reg. "Seems we are in the same boat you and me, Gordie. Same boat.

What a pair."

"I always thought you had family, wife and kids; sorry we didn't see much of each other over the years Reg."

"She left me after eight months of marriage," says Reg. "Never heard from her again. So I never bothered, wasn't worth the hassle. Women! Anyway, Christmas? Do you fancy

The Lodge?"

Christmas comes. There was something alien about staying in an hotel, getting dressed in a suit and tie for dinner, being waited on. "This is the life," says Gordon to Reg as they sit by the roaring fire after the turkey-with-all-the-trimmings dinner. Sipping brandies. Wearing paper hats. They turn together and look out at the ocean, the Atlantic rolling gently in on the icy white sands at the couples walking arm in arm along the beach, in red knitted toques and knee-high boots. At the children running back and forth to the icy waves, shrieking then running back to the dunes, hiding behind the ice laden grasses, rushing out screaming in joy and thrill, as only children can do.

"Lucky," says Gordon.

"Yes," says Reg, "but things aren't always what they seem."

In the eight weeks following Christmas, the two men prepare for their trip. Gordon's passport arrives. He keeps it in the oak desk and every day or so; he takes it out and turns the pristine pages, thinking how proud his father would be, and his mother too. Or would they? Would they think he was disturbing things, things that should be left just as they are, hidden within suitcases or desk drawers, or with lawyers in far-off lands? It didn't matter now; the decision was made, and Gordon and Reg were all geared up for the trip.

Reg booked them into the Radisson Plaza on the Avenida Vitacura, quite close to the offices of the lawyers he had made arrangements with. Gordon was glad to have Reg as his friend and ally on this, otherwise he just wouldn't have known where to start. He guesses he would have got on a plane in Halifax and got off in Chile and just taken it from there.

But Reg was more methodical. He knew that they would need all the time they could get to talk with people and sort things out.

In the meantime, they both signed up for Spanish for Beginners through Parks and Recreation. The classes are held in their old High School from seven to nine on Wednesday evenings beginning January 5th.

In some ways, Bagpipes for Beginners being held in the music room down the hall doesn't hurt things at all. It seems to add to the experience, to the uniqueness of it all. Gordon is beginning to find his life has taken on a whole new level. He is doing things and going places he never dreamed of. Evening classes were certainly never part of his life plan.

As he stumbles through *hola* to *adios* on night one to *a correos* and *una parada de taxis* by week three, he knows that by the time he and Reg leave Halifax, they should at least be able to greet people and ask for a taxi.

When the time comes, the morning before the night flight, Gordon drives Pea over to Joslyn's place. It is an uneasy parting, the two have never been separated before. Gordon finds Joslyn making dog food for Louie and Pea. She is grinding ginger root with spinach and zucchini. She has meat and bones from the farm and the kitchen smells like Gordon's used to smell, when his mother was alive, cooking stews for him.

"They'll be getting it some good," he says.

"This? Oh, this is the norm in this house, take a look at these." She opens the oven door where six dozen cookies are baking. "Banana, sardine and molasses," she says. "Some good all right."

"I'm going to leave you with this," says Gordon. "It's to cover her costs and in case you have to take her to the vet or something. Anything you need." He places a sealed envelope containing two thousand dollars in one hundred-dollar bills on the side table. Even that doesn't make him feel any better about leaving his one constant and loyal companion and friend, Pea. "Be a good girl," he says, "I'll be home before you know it." He looks up at Joslyn, "I'll email you," he says, "let you know how I'm doing; I can text you too, now you've shown me how, even post some photos on Facebook. And thank you again, you are making this possible you know."

Gordon and Joslyn hug, a tight squeeze, and then he turns on his heels and leaves. Trying not to look back. Trying not to hear the sad cries of his sweet Pea. It sounds just like the seals moaning out on the ice.

8.

The drive to Halifax's Stanfield International Airport is uneventful. Reg has arranged for one of his employees to drive them, in his Lexus, thereby saving the worry of parking and leaving the car for eight weeks. They know they are in for a twenty-hour trip all told, counting check-in times and the change in Toronto, but flight AC 615 takes off on time at 20.25. Gordon, who has never flown before, is surprised that the plane feels just like getting on a bus. They have seats in the front section and as soon as they are settled the cabin crew come around with newspapers and coffee.

The change at Toronto Pearson takes Gordon by surprise, but Reg has passes for the Maple Leaf Lounge where, again, they are treated like VIPs until it's time for AC092 to Santiago.

Gordon feels Reg look across at him as the cabin crew tuck them into their first-class pods, offering pyjamas and hot chocolate. He smiles back at Reg, hoping they are not on some wild goose chase, wishing for only good to come from this journey into the unknown, putting all the uncertainties to rest.

Within half an hour, they are asleep and when the lights are turned up with the smell of breakfast, they wake and look across the aisle at each other. "Are we nearly there then?" says Gordon.

Reg laughs, "I guess we are, that didn't hurt one bit, did it."

The procedure on landing in Santiago takes them by surprise. "We are on vacation.

Holiday," says Reg, when an immigration officer asks the purpose of the visit. He had already told Gordon to say as little as possible.

The immigration officials look at Gordon's Canadian passport and say, 'Pliss, come this way pliss, Sir."

"I will come too, if I may," says Reg.

"Ah, no, only Mr. Drummond," says the immigration official.

"But I am his lawyer," says Reg. Which turned out to be the wrong thing to say as for ten hours the two men are questioned. Their baggage gone through item by item. Kept separate, neither knew just what the other was saying, or not saying. Gordon heeded Reg's advice and said very little, not letting on he understood a bit of Spanish. Slowly coming to realise that his father's name must be on file. Something to do with income tax and the mine.

"Do you know Andrew Drummond?" says the immigration guy in the navy-blue hat with gold braid. "Father to you?"

Gordon said one word, "Dead."

And that seemed to be it. Reg and Gordon were put together in another room where they were asked where they were staying, and what their plans were. Reg did the talking. "We are staying here in the city for one week. We want to see the place my friend's father lived, so we will go to Valparaiso after one week. We are on holiday, but we look for family too. Is that okay?"

They are released into bright sunshine. Unshaven, sweating and eager for food and a shower. The taxi takes them to the Radisson. "But you didn't arrive," says the receptionist at the front desk, "your rooms are no longer available, we just have one room left."

"We were delayed," says Reg, "not our fault. Not yours either, we'll take what you have.

It is for one week, yes?"

"Sir."

As the two men close the door on room 317, they breathe deeply. Almost in unison. "Never expected any of that," says Gordon.

"I should have thought," says Reg. "If there was any shady business going on, then your dad would be blacklisted, but I would have thought after more than twenty years..."

"Let's not worry about it," says Gordon. "Do you want the shower first?"

And with that they slip into an easy sharing of space. Making coffee and tea for each other at the room's kitchen bar area. Ordering room service and lying back on the two king sized beds in undershorts watching the news in Spanish on the TV.

By evening they are ready to take in some sights. Before they go Gordon sends Joslyn an email from his new iPad: 'Hi Jos, we've arrived. Bit of a delay and upset at the airport here but all okay now. We are at the hotel I told you about and gave you the numbers for. But you've got our cell phone numbers if something crops up. Kisses for Pea. G.'

He thought after he'd hit send that maybe he should

have included kisses for her too, but it was too late and anyhow, Reg was raring to go hit the town.

They started in the hotel bar. Glitzy; mirrors, crystal chandeliers. Old, faded sepia photos around the wall in gilded frames. Photos of the British era when Chile was more English than England. Just like parts of India too. With street names like Cambridge Road and Hereford Boulevard. "I had no idea," says Gordon to Reg, "no idea that the place used to be so British." "It does make you think, doesn't it," says Reg, "how much things have changed in the past, even over the past fifty years."

They sip their cold beers sitting out on the verandah on rattan chairs under the stars and marvel at the warm temperatures. "Of course, we are in the southern hemisphere, the seasons are the other way around, aren't they?"

Reg doesn't reply, he has his eyes closed and he's breathing deeply. Then he says, "You know, none of this would be happening if your dad hadn't died leaving you with this mystery, we wouldn't be sitting here now, would we? Makes you think."

"Indeed," says Gordon, "and we have tomorrow to look forward to, too. What time is the appointment?'

"Eleven," says Reg. "Time to start really taking the lid off. Do you still want to? There is always time to back right out now?"

"No going back," says Gordon. "And maybe we should just sit here for a while, not worry about looking for night life tonight. Tomorrow may turn out to be a big day."

9.

The offices of Snrs. Jose and Gladstone on Avenue Santa Lucia are old school. Reg said he was expecting all glass and steel. Instead, the colonial building has a facade of columns and mellow stonework like something out of a book of architectural history. The two men took a taxi, even though the law offices appeared to be close by, the concierge assured them the road was 'very very busy, taxi is best,' and so they were guided by him.

They climb out of the taxi and look up at the impressive building and then at each other. "Jeez Reg, how much is this going to cost?" says Gordon.

"Don't know, but we'll ask that early on. First one hour meeting two hundred dollars. It may be enough for us."

They are directed to the second floor, no elevator, but a gentle curved staircase with highly polished brass handrail and rich, dark red carpet on the stair treads held in place by Victorian stair rods. They remind Gordon of the rods his mother took up from the stairs back home. They have the same acorn carvings at each end. He has no time to wonder where they came from, or why she took them up. They reach the 2nd floor and are shown into a large office with French doors opening out onto a balcony with views across the city and towards the mountains. A man stands on the balcony with his back to Reg and Gordon.

He turns. "Good morning," he says in a perfect English accent. "Bill Gladstone, senior partner, so glad to meet you. Finally. You must be Reginald Conrad," he says to Gordon.

"No," says Gordon, smiling, relieved that he wouldn't have to resort to his meagre Spanish, "this here is Reg, my lawyer and friend, I am Gordon Drummond."

Bill Gladstone points to a seating area of the office with deep leather couches and a brass topped coffee table. "Shall we? And please, call me Bill."

As the three men settle into the leather couches, the door opens and a tray of teacups, tea pot and a plate of ginger cookies appears in the arms of a young man. "Thank you, Jorge," says Bill Gladstone. "Hope you all like tea, or would you rather have coffee or something cold."

"Tea is fine for us, ain't that right, Gordie," says Reg, winking. "Yup, tea's good," says Gordon. "A touch of the old country?"

"Indeed," says Bill. "But I was born here, my parents too. It was my grandparents who were the settlers. I do go back to England from time to time. I went to boarding school there, then to Oxford and on to Law School after that. But I missed this place. It doesn't compare with England. Have you been?"

"What," says Gordon, "to the UK? Oh my, oh my, oh my, I've never been further than Halifax Nova Scotia. I had to get my first passport to come here and I'm sixty-two years old." The three men laugh. A genuine laugh that indicates common ground.

"Oh yes, by the way," says Reg, "the immigration people have kept our passports, all tied up with our reason for the visit, can we ask you to look into that for us?"

"They'll be fine," says Bill, "I'll take care of that as part of this case file if that's okay.

Now, maybe we should get down to business, then I'll take you somewhere really good for lunch. Don't worry, that will be off-tab, it is just so refreshing to meet a couple of fellows like yourselves. Maybe I'll take a trip to your part of the world at some point, and you can return the favour, I hear the lobster is very good."

"You can say that again," says Reg, "but the industry is suffering, just like everything else."

"Indeed," says Bill. "Now, let's take a look at what you wanted to see me about shall we."

He pulls a mahogany cart towards him. It has three red box files piled on the top. Below is a cabinet with the door open. Inside is a wooden box about the size of a shoe box.

"I've been in touch with a small firm of lawyers up in Valparaiso," he says. "They sent these items down by courier last week, I felt I should do a bit of research on your behalf, in advance of your arrival. I've actually already run up quite an account for you."

Reg looks at Gordon, then back at Bill. "How much?" he says.

"We're already over six thousand US dollars," says Bill, "but you may not need much more than we have managed to collate already, this consultation is included in that amount and any of my time in the few days you are here, I'll be happy to answer questions."

Gordon nods at Reg. "Sounds good," he says. "We just don't want to break the bank; this project may turn out to cost more than it's worth."

"I think you'll be happy with what I've found," says Bill. "The only problem is people— there are people who may find this upsetting. Your father had two lives, Mr. Drummond, sorry, Gordon. Two lives. He kept them both separate, very cleverly, I might add."

"We've already gathered that much," interjects Reg. "With the information we found back home, passports, references to a mine. And photographs. Photos of a woman, or women and a child or children."

"I hate to tell you this, Gordon, but I suspect you may already be prepared for a bombshell. You see, your father was, in fact, a bigamist."

10.

The taxi takes the three men to the Aquesta Coco seafood restaurant on Andres Bello about ten minutes from the law offices. It is 1.30 and Reg's stomach has rumbled for twenty minutes. Bill took the hint, ordered the taxi, and now they are seated at a round table in a quiet corner, overlooking a tree-lined boulevard. The facade of the restaurant is not dissimilar to that of Bill's law offices. "Same architect," he tells them, in response to their quizzical expressions. "His work is everywhere; did some work for The National Gallery in London, too."

Gordon sips his tall green glass of bottled water, pushing the lemon slice out of the way with his tongue. He studies the menu, "Not exactly MacDonald's is it?"

Bill laughs. "It is good," he says, "everything is good. They do a sampler if you'd like."

Gordon orders the sampler for an appetizer, Reg orders the king crab, following Bill's lead. For their entree they each settle for catch of the day, swordfish, although Reg's attention is drawn to the eel. "We catch eels in Nova Scotia," he tells Bill, "down along the Eastern Shore. They have the seal of approval from Her Majesty the Queen."

Bill nods, "I will have to visit, it sounds an extraordinary place. Bet you fellows are missing it all ready."

Gordon hasn't thought about what he's missing, until Bill mentions the words. Pea's face jumps into his mind immediately and he says, "Can you excuse me for just one moment, I need to check something." He pulls his iPad from his attaché case and looks at the photos of Pea. Her dark brown eyes like melting velvet, her pink nose showing through her short white coat. He wallows hard, then looks up at the table as the appetizers arrive. "Sorry about that," he says, "just something I had to do."

"So, Bill," says Reg, munching his crab, "where do we go from here?"

"The mine is in trouble," says Bill, "not financial trouble, that is well secured. No it's all this new environmental stuff. The mine has been taken to court by the environmental department of the local government up there for non-compliance."

"What can I do?" says Gordon.

"Your father was the owner," says Bill, "but when he left, over twenty years ago, he signed over ownership to his daughter, Perdita Drummond and her son."

There is a stillness and a silence around the table. Gordon looks up from his plate. He sees the gilded framed mirrors around the restaurant walls, reflecting lights, blue skies, sun, dazzling him with images of himself. The table appears to rise and then fall. Reg and Bill look at him.

"I have a sister?" is all he can say. "Perdita? That's what Dad wanted to call Pea when we got her. So he called her Perdie. It all makes sense now. He gave all that up to come back home. Didn't he?"

Bill nods. He says nothing.

Reg reaches across for Gordon's hand. "We'll get it all

sorted, Gordie," he says, giving his hand a squeeze.

The lunch is memorable in many ways. That's how Reg retells it later, when the trip is over, when he talks about remembering most of the words spoken with each serving of the five- course lunch. The dessert of Lucuma Cake, described as a traditional meringue lucuma or eggfruit frost cake filled with a crunchy and soft meringue and lucuma cream. He says he still has no idea what lucuma is but will always remember the feeling that he was transported to a different world. Thanks to Gordon. Thanks to Gordon's dad dying and leaving a mess to be sorted out.

They say goodbye to Bill back at the law offices. Bill has copied the documents onto a memory stick in addition to packing many things into one box file for Gordon. Reg keeps the memory stick as back up, "Just in case," he says.

Gordon understands. After they were split up in immigration, he wants to be double sure that nothing gets lost in translation this time.

They have five days to kill while staying in the Radisson before heading to Valparaiso. Gordon sees little reason to waste the time, "Let's be tourists, for the next few days."

Reg agrees, "But not today," he says. They spend what is left of that life-changing day in their room at the Radisson, sifting through documents and talking.

"Who would have thought it?" Gordon says.

"I reckon nine out of ten people have a secret life. You'd be surprised at some of the things I have to deal with in my job."

"I still wonder if Mom knew. I guess I'll never really find that out now."

There is a sadness in Gordon's voice, but also a new-found exhilaration. He is thinking that tomorrow, out in this city as a tourist, he could be walking the same streets as his father before him. That he's getting a taste of his father's other life. He wonders now why it had to be such a great big secret.

He also wonders who is this sister? Was she the woman at the funeral? Through the afternoon and evening of that eventful day, sitting on the sunny balcony of the Radisson Santiago, Gordon phones Joslyn, Reg phones the office, and they reassure themselves that all is well back on the icy south shore of Nova Scotia.

The following morning, they leave their valuables and the paperwork in the safe in the hotel room and head on out to explore Santiago. Bill has already given them some ideas, "If you're interested in art and architecture," he said, "you'll probably enjoy wandering the cobbled streets of Santiago's older barrios, but if you are out in the mid-day heat, then maybe Parque Quinta Normal would be a good bet, it houses over a half dozen museums within an incredible maze of greenery." He'd scribbled down a few places on a table napkin and Reg has it in his pocket.

But it's the Cerro San Cristobal that Reg and Gordon head for first. Reg has read aloud the description from the brochure over breakfast, *towering over the Chilean capital, this hill- hugging park is a recreational oasis with public pools, botanical gardens, and breathtaking views of both the city and the Andean peaks—smog permitting. Santiguans come here to jog, bike, and hike. Tourists come to ride the rickety funicular up to the hilltop Virgin Mary statue and sip on mote con huesillo while taking in the panorama.*

So that's what Gordon and Reg do, they ride the rickety funicular, a mountain railway rising steeply from the city until they reach the top. They get out, breathe deeply and look way down over the city partly cloaked in smog. They use their smart phones to take photos, of the view, of each other, and then like kids, hold out their phones to take photos of themselves, poking out their tongues like fourteen-year-olds do for Facebook. Laughing. Arms around each other in this new-found experience and friendship.

When they return to their hotel, just after sunset, they find a courier has delivered their passports to the front desk.

<h1 style="text-align:center">11.</h1>

Planning the trip to Valparaiso has not been without difficulty. Initially they were not sure why they are going, and why for so long. Gordon, felt, right from the day they decided to go to Chile, that if there were things needing his attention, then a couple of weeks would not be enough.

They'd double checked the type of air tickets and felt confident that, if need be, they could cut the trip short and just go home.

Valparaiso is only seventy miles northwest of Santiago. Gordon and Reg, after a couple of days in the capital, wondered if a car rental would be a good idea. Bill visited them part way through the week and suggested it would be better taking a bus or even a van taxi and renting a car when they got there, that is, if they felt they really needed a car. "Valparaiso is quite a large city," said Bill, "you may find it's too stressful. If I could, I'd come along with you, really. But I have a big case coming up next week. If it gets an adjournment, I'll let you know. Now you have my cell phone number and I have yours. Let me know how you make out."

They opt for the bus. It turns out to be a comfortable long-distance coach with a washroom, but a luggage restriction. Bill comes to their aid at the last moment saying, "I'll get it sent out to you, let me know for sure where you will be staying."

"We've decided against a hotel, Bill," says Reg. "Because it's a long stay we wanted somewhere we could spread out, invite people round if need be. More a home away from home kinda thing."

"Yes," says Gordon, "there's this website called homeaway.com." He smiles, so glad he got himself up to speed on computer searching and the like. "The one we've booked has got three bedrooms and three bathrooms." Gordon and Reg begin to laugh. "So we'll have loads of space if you do want to join us."

"Wow! Where is it?" says Bill.

"Somewhere called Cerro Alegre," says Reg, reading from his printout, "apparently a world heritage part of the city, well placed, good views and plenty of parking. Looks nice. We've booked it for six weeks. Got a good deal."

"When did you book it?" says Bill.

"Just before we left home, we looked at hotels, and well, we are not really hotel kind of people. We want to do some cooking, shop in the local markets, get a feel for what it's like to live here. They are letting us have it for $500 a week."

"Yes," adds Gordon, "and if we feel like taking a trip to another area, we can leave our stuff there, and travel light. I'm hoping this new, yet to meet, family of mine will be able to spend time with us too."

Bill assures them that all will be well as he says goodbye. "If all Nova Scotians are as easy going as you two, it must be one lovely place to live. But enjoy Valparaiso. It used to be big in English heritage, many immigrants settled there. You'll see some of the traditions have lingered. There's actually an Irish Pub I think, that's probably about the closest to what you have back home. Still, enjoy, let me know if there's anything you need. And I will make sure you get these," he says, pointing to the suitcases at his feet.

The bus ride suits the two men perfectly, they stow their one bag each in the luggage hold and board the bus with small backpacks containing bottles of water, snacks, their passports and travel documents. They sit back and watch as the country passes by. It is eleven in the morning and the roads are busy.

"Bill was right about a car rental," says Gordon, pointing out the cars flashing by the bus at top speed.

Reg nods. He watches through the tinted windows. He stretches, finds the foot-rest under the seat in front. The highway running out of Santiago is hectic. There is much concrete and merging of traffic. "Yes, I understand now what Bill was saying. I'm so glad we didn't rent a car."

After about half an hour they leave the city and find themselves on a twinned highway, much like highway 103 back home. It is bordered by scrubland and then foothills of mountains. The distant hills are a pale purple and puffs of white clouds skit across the sky. Reg looks up through the Velox in the roof of the bus. He says to Gordon, "Can you believe we are doing this?"

"Funny," says Gordon, "I was thinking the same thing. Look we're at the road toll, does it remind you of the Cobequid Pass?"

After a couple of hours, with the two men watching the scenery, napping and sipping water, they begin to enter the outskirts of Valparaiso. The roads are lined with tall trees, tin shacks of a shanty town, rickety fences held together with torn tarps. As they begin to descend Gordon says, "Look. The sea."

"I see it," says Reg. "It's the South Pacific."

"Seems these little shacks have the best view," says Gordon, "can't help wondering now, if we've done the right thing. This family stuff is sure bothering me."

But as they get closer to the city itself they see pretty, pale pink fences. Houses painted pale gold and olive green.

"Wouldn't look amiss in Newfoundland, B'y," says Reg with a wink as he slips into a Newfoundland accent.

The road surface changes to old cobblestones and houses looking like those in the American Deep south, with ornate balustrades over tiny balconies.

"It's quiet," says Reg, "do you think it's siesta time?"

"Si, si," says a voice from the seat in front. "Siesta, si." And a shiny head pops up and smiles a wide white smile.

The bus drops them outside a small white church. They are thankful to get off, stretch their legs and retrieve their bags. Reg phones the number he's been given for the apartment. "Ye wait. Be right with ye," a Scots voice tells him. So they sit on a park bench by the small white church which also seems to act as a bus terminus. Gordon studies the graffiti on walls up and down the street. "It doesn't look very prosperous, does it?" he says.

"Hmmm," says Reg, "we may not be staying as long as we thought then." Within minutes a small white van pulls up beside them and a gaunt man wearing tattered shorts and a Tartan- Army football t-shirt.

"Guid timing," he says, "I'm Jock McLeod, I've got yer keys here. I'll tak yer to the flat.

It's just aroond the corner here."

Set in an alleyway, between the old crumbling small stores and houses is a double iron gate. Jock unlocks the gate. "This is key number one," he says. "It's not complicated, there are only two keys, one for the gate, and one for the main door."

The apartments are modern and well equipped; not what Gordon and Reg are used to back home. Jock tells them, "Ye've got my number if ye need anything, there's a stack o' leaflets and that, telling ye what's what o'er there, and there's a little shop for groceries just across the road, it opens at aroond four, but ye'll find some stuff to get ye started. Bread, tea, coffee, milk, that kinda thing already here."

"Thank you," says Reg. "Is it easy to find out where things are, to get around, you know?"

"Och, aye," says Jock. 'If ye need the gay bars, ye've to go a couple of blocks over." And with that, he was gone.

Gordon and Reg collapsed onto the large sofa in guffaws of laughter. "I'll get the tea kettle on," says Reg, still laughing.

"I'll get a load of wash going as soon as we've unpacked. Be good to get some of these sweaty clothes washed, won't it?"

"Listen to you," says Reg, "no wonder Jock thought we were gay." "Ha, yeah, funny," says Gordon, "and there is internet, right?" "Supposed to be," says Reg, "I'll check it out."

With mugs of hot tea in their hands and the washing machine underway, they still can't get an internet connection. "I'll call Jock," says Reg.

"Och aye," says Jock, "I should-a-said, ye'll need the passcode, it's scotlandthebrave all lowercase. Okay?"

"Got it, many thanks," says Reg. He calls to Gordon, "I've got it, just connecting now."

Between them they've taken over three hundred photographs, mostly bright colourful street scenes, views from the bus, a couple of goofy ones of each other. Nothing spectacular. But Gordon wants to send a couple to Joslyn for her to show Pea. He also wants to email her.

A message comes straight back, "Pea still has fleas."

"So sorry," writes Gordon, "I thought we'd got them all, so sorry, did she give them to Louie?"

"Funny," writes back Jos, "I think she got them from Louie in the first place. Don't worry I'm taking care of them. How's things?"

"Things are good, we've moved to the coast, in an apartment now, very nice, better than a hotel, three bedrooms, three bathrooms, when are you coming? (joke) we can see the Pacific from here."

Joslyn doesn't reply. Gordon wonders if he's offended her.

Reg says, "The internet connection dropped out. Maybe we should try later. Are you aware that it's more than dogs have brought you two closer?"

Gordon shrugs, "I guess," he says. "I've also been thinking back to the funeral." "Huh?"

"Yup, I can see more clearly now, black figures shuffling

through the snow, like fleas through Pea's white coat. Reg, there was more than just one woman."

By four o'clock the world outside the apartment complex starts to come back to life. The small stores open their shutters, and a bustle of activity begins to hum. "What do you think?" says Reg. "Shall we go exploring?"

"Well, yes, why not," says Gordon, "but shouldn't I try and make contact with this woman first?"

"I thought you might want to catch your breath after the bus ride, get your bearings, look for some groceries for making supper first, then you might begin to feel more human, and be more able to handle this. You know this is something you have to do on your own, right?"

Gordon does know. He's still not sure how he's going to go about it, so for Reg to take a walk around the area, see what's what, get a few supplies might not be a bad idea. "Give me ten minutes, okay?"

When Reg returns, Gordon is waiting on the doorstep. Flushed. "I did it," he says. "What?" says Reg.

"I phoned her. When I was all alone in there, it was absolutely quiet except for the swishing of the washing machine. So I phoned the number Bill gave us."

"What did she say?"

"She's coming over at ten tomorrow morning."

"Jeez, that's the worst bit over, I'd say, well done, Gordie, what did she sound like?" "Soft spoken," says Gordon, "just like Dad. Now, where are we off to?"

"I'm impressed, really. How about we forget about groceries and head down to the waterfront? I'm really dying to see the Pacific."

It is more of a trek from the apartment than they first thought, after a couple of blocks they spot a line of taxis and ask the first one to take them down to the front. "Esplanade?" asks the driver. "Si," says Gordon, more than happy to make use of the eight-week course in Bridgewater. "Si, por favor."

The taxi drops them at a wide palm-tree-lined road. Busy with traffic, tall, ornate colonial style buildings on one side and a promenade on the other. Valparaiso citizens were promenading; couples arm in arm letting the sea breezes cool them down, babies in strollers with their mothers in tight-fitting capri pants and bespangled t-shirts. Youngsters with school bags on their backs, kicking stones and delaying going home to do their homework. It is a busy spot.

Reg and Gordon take photographs then sit on a bench looking out over a glittering ocean and talk again about what is to come.

"It WAS her," says Gordon. "What was?"

"At Dad's funeral, it was her. She said so. She said she was sorry she didn't speak. Sorry that she had returned here without seeing me."

"So what will you talk about tomorrow?"

"I don't know," says Gordon, "I know how foolish that might sound, but I honestly don't know."

"Will you want me to leave you to it?"

"I thought about that," says Gordon, "of course I don't.

We are in this together. Well kind of, I wouldn't have done any of this without you. But I will not introduce you as a lawyer, just a friend."

"Not JUST a friend, I hope," says Reg, slinging his arm across Gordon's shoulder, "good friends I hope. I can keep ducking back to the kitchen, make coffee, put cookies on a plate, that kind of thing. If it goes well, we could take her to lunch, we can look somewhere up on the internet tonight."

"All sounds good, Reg, thanks, so we will still have to get a few things in for tomorrow then. But first let's find something to eat down here, then pick some stuff up at one of those stores near the apartment on our way back."

They find a small eatery. Reg practices his Spanish this time, but they don't get the pizza he ordered, they get battered deep fried octopus with French fries on the side. They laugh and decide to give it a try. "Not bad," they agree, washing it down with a cold beer that doesn't get lost in translation. They ask the waiter to order a taxi for them when they're done. The taxi takes them back to the corner near the apartment where the small convenience store is still open. They buy peaches and eggs and some kind of cookies that they think Perdita might like.

The internet is working when they get in. Joslyn has received some of the photos, she says they make her laugh and suggests that they could try Skype another time, then Pea could listen to Gordon, she thinks the dog is missing him. "Not as much as I am missing her," murmurs Gordon before his head hits the pillow.

It is their first night in Valparaiso.

<h1 style="text-align:center">12.</h1>

Gordon is up early. He makes coffee and sits on the balcony, watching the city come to life. Small delivery trucks rattle up and down cobbled streets dropping off cases of Coca Cola, milk and assorted fruits and vegetables. He smells freshly baked bread and is about to go in search of its source when Reg stumbles out of his bedroom door, "You up then already?"

"Ha, of course, couldn't sleep. This is exciting stuff. Don't you think?" "Indeed, do you smell fresh bread?"

"Yes, I was just going hunting for it, do you want to go?"

"No, that's okay, you go, I'll get a shower and see what clothes are fit to wear."

Gordon grabs the keys from the counter and puts his wallet in his back pocket. Reg stops him, "I've been told it's best not to put your wallet there," he says, "apparently there are pick- pockets."

"Right," says Gordon, feeling the wind being taken out of his sails. "I'll just take a bit of cash. Ten thousand pesos should do it?"

"I should say so, I think five hundred is about the same as our dollar. You should take a bit more in case you see something else."

"I'll get used to it, we will need to find a bank soon though, I'd rather use cash, wouldn't you?"

When Gordon gets back with two fresh white loaves and a carton of mango juice, Reg is showered and has tidied up the apartment. "Gotta look nice for the lady visitor," he says. "Did you bring anything for her from home?"

"I did as a matter of fact," says Gordon. "I brought her a small bottle of maple syrup and a carved loon. I have no idea what she might like, but that's all I've got."

"Plenty, and perfect I'd say. Now we'd better get breakfast and clear away before she gets here. Is she coming alone?"

"Good question. Don't know. We'll soon find out."

As the clock slips around to ten, Gordon gets anxious. He stands up, walks the floor, out to the balcony, back to the chairs on the far wall. Stands and looks at the artwork on the walls— water colours of sail boats. Sits down again. Rearranges the tourist brochures on the coffee table. The time is now ten after ten.

"You did say ten?" says Reg.

"Yup, woman's privilege I suppose, either that or she's inherited the Nova Scotia time- keeping gene."

"You gave her the address?" "Yup, and the phone number." "What about the gate?"

"The gate?"

"Yes, you need the key to get through the gate."

"I think there's a bell, or a voice thing, isn't there?"

At twenty-five minutes past ten the access phone rings.

Gordon goes down to the gate. A pale metallic blue Mercedes convertible is parked awaiting admission. He opens the gate. The car doesn't move. Out steps a tall angular woman with long dark hair. She is wearing large sunglasses, a red striped cotton blouse and jeans.

"Hello Gordon," she says. He moves towards her. Slowly. She opens her arms. "I am Perdita," she says.

Gordon is not used to physical expressions of affection, but he is drawn to this woman and hugs her. "Hello," he says, "it is good to meet you."

She brings the car into the parking space, locks it and together they walk up to the apartment where Reg is waiting with tea laid out on the dining table. Cups, saucers with spoons. Small plates for cookies and a blue bowl of peaches in the centre of the table.

"Perdita, this is my friend Reg from Mahone Bay," he says. "Reg, this is Perdita. My sister." It feels strange to say the words. He looks at her and she smiles. It is his father's smile, and he has no doubt she is his sister.

"You've both got some catching up to do," says Reg. "I just have to go out for about an hour. Bank, Post Office, that kind of thing. I won't be too long. Then maybe we can all go for lunch; I understand the city is going through a culinary rebirth." Reg blushes, wondering if he's said too much, but covers it up by saying, "I was reading all about it in the Good Food Guide."

"I know a great place," says Perdita, "it is a little way out, and maybe if we could all get into my little car with no trouble, I can drive us."

With Reg out of the apartment an awkward silence settles over Gordon and Perdita. They sit opposite each other at the dining table. Studying each other's features. Looking for signs.

"You look like him," Gordon says. "As do you," says

Perdita.

"You must have missed him when he left," says Gordon. "As must you, just a small boy."

The conversation is one of empathy and understanding. "I'm glad you are here," she says. "I'm glad too, I have no-one now."

"But your friend?" Perdita points to the door.

"Reg and I were at elementary school together. We've known each other all our lives.

He's not my partner or anything like that." "Were you never married?"

"No, I looked after Mom. Then when she passed, it was Dad. I've never left home. How sad is that?"

"Not sad. It is good. You are a good son. I hope I was a good daughter too." Gordon refreshes the teacups and offers Perdita a cookie. She takes one and nibbles the edges. Gordon can see she is as nervous as he and wonders how he can help overcome it.

"Hang on," he says, "I have something for you." He goes into the bedroom and comes back with a gift bag. "Just small things," he says, not wanting to cause embarrassment, "a couple of things from home, I thought you might like."

Perdita draws out the bottle of maple syrup first. "You have brought this all this way?

Thank you so much. Papa often talked about how he missed it." She put her hand to her mouth as if she'd made a blunder, "sorry, I did not mean..."

"It's okay you know," says Gordon. "It's absolutely fine. So he was Papa to you and he was Dad to me. Seems he was two different people. One foot in one world, and the other in another. I have his old passports; he wasn't just here in Chile you know."

"No? Did he not come home to you every year, at Christmas time? He left us here and said he had to go away."

"I think he was in New York each Christmas," Gordon says, shrugging his shoulders, not knowing what more he could say.

Perdita plunges her hand back into the gift bag. "Ah, this is wonderful. I know what it is.

A loon," she says, "like Looniberg."

Gordon laughs. "Lunenburg, I don't think they are connected. But it is a beautiful bird. It has a haunting cry. It carries its babies on its back across the water."

"I have something for you too," she pulls a velvet bag out of her purse. Gordon recognises it as similar to the small bags in the suitcase on top of the armoire. "We found these recently, when going back through Papa's trunk. We never had the key before, then just before his death, it came by FedEx. Gordon draws back the silken strings of the bag and pulls out a silver watch on a chain. "This was his?" he says.

"Yes, open the back," she says in a whisper.

Gordon flips open the silver watch back and there lies a golden curl. His. He knows it is his. He cannot help himself as the tears tumble down his cheeks, he sobs. He turns his head away in embarrassment, then when he looks back, he sees Perdita crying too. Heavy mascara running down her face.

"We need to get out for a while," he says, "this is really

quite overwhelming. It is actually almost unbelievable. But together, slowly, I think we can put the pieces together."

When Reg comes back, he finds the two sitting on the balcony talking about birds and bird watching, something Gordon has never mentioned before. "How's it going?" he says.

"Good, how did you get on at the bank?"

"Oh fine," says Reg, "good job I took my passport though, apparently I needed ID. Anyway, I've got cash, shall we go to lunch?"

Reg climbs into the back of the convertible and doubles his knees up under him, "It's a good job I'm a skinny guy," he says, laughing.

"It is not too far," says Perdita, but this not a good idea, I will call another car." She flips open a silver cell phone and rattles out rapid Spanish. "We wait, five minutes only," she says. "Other car will come."

The gold Mercedes limo glides around the corner without Reg or Gordon hearing a sound. "Here it is," says Perdita. "I will leave my car here and we will go together," she says to Reg and Gordon. "Gracias, José," she says to the driver. "Bella Vista por favor."

A ten-minute drive takes them to a higher level, a good residential area, and a boulevard of designer stores and high-class restaurants. José pulls up to a place set back from the rest.

There are potted geraniums on the steps, sunflowers in the small front flower beds and the sign above the awning says 'Drummonds'.

Perdita sees the look on Gordon's face and smiles, tentatively. "It is my son's restaurant," she says. "He is a chef."

Gordon is speechless. He is not sure he can cope with many more surprises. But it is with a feeling of premonition that he enters the restaurant. He doesn't notice the 'closed' sign on the door, but Reg does. As they leave the bright sunlight and walk into the richly decorated restaurant, they see every table filled with people. The people stand and begin to clap, and say "Welcome Gordon Drummond, welcome, bien venidos." Perdita walks to the far end of the room, the people sit, and she shows Reg and Gordon to a table at the centre where her son, Eduardo, stands. Gordon is speechless, he is the spitting image of Andrew.

"Hi," he says, "at long last we get to meet. You are my Uncle Gordon."

Reg pulls out a chair and sits down, hoping to get everyone settled. This wasn't the light chatty lunch he had in mind, but 'when in Rome,' he tells himself.

"Hello everyone," says Gordon, before he sits down, "it is lovely to be here. This is my friend Reg from Canada."

This starts a whole lot of 'welcomes' all over again and clapping until Gordon sits down with Reg on his left, Perdita on his right, and Eduardo opposite.

The food begins to appear. Gordon recognises so many dishes. Just like his father's suppers he had made ready each evening for Gordon coming in from work. The dishes with the eggplants, the fancy desserts with unpronounceable fruit. Deep rich wine and soft freshly made bread on the side.

Gordon wonders if he'll wake up soon and find himself back at Indian Point surrounded by ice and snow. For a brief moment feels homesick, as if he has landed on some alien planet. But he also begins to get a stronger feeling of the life his father led, and what he had to leave behind to come home twenty years ago. These people, so colourful and exciting and obviously successful. So happy. Yes, that was the feeling in the room, one of happiness. No incriminations. No questions about why, or why not.

Gordon reaches for Reg's hand under the table, and gives it a squeeze. Reg grins at him and squeezes back. "Okay?" he mouths.

Gordon nods. "Okay," he mouths back. And he knows that for the time being anyway, things are really okay. He has no idea what tomorrow will bring, what affect the court case about the gold mine will have on him, or what other skeletons will drop from the sky, but for now, all is fine.

Perdita turns to him and says, "We go to my house after this, you may wish to Skype your friends back home. Talk to your little dog, yes?"

And Gordon wonders how in the hell she could read his mind.

13.

Gordon can't remember all the details of that first day of meeting his sister. The afternoon is as blurred as his dad's funeral and the weeks that followed were. A small group of the extended family went back to Perdita's house before Reg and Gordon returned to the rented apartment. He does remember the feeling of visiting her house for the first time. A mixed feeling of jealousy and pride.

The house stands high above the city with wide views of the Pacific from every window. The limo tires crunch the gravel driveway. Gordon watches the palm trees and other foliage he has only seen on PBS's nature documentaries. He feels that he is entering even deeper into another world. A mysterious, even wondrous, place from which there could be no return. He asks himself if his father ever felt the same pleasure in entrapment. Wanting to leave and wanting to stay. All at the same time.

Reg takes photographs with his smart phone, "Unbelievable," he says, "what do you think?" Gordon doesn't reply. He blots his watering eyes with a Kleenex, as if he's clearing them for a better view, using it as a pretence for his emotions. Still wondering if his mother ever knew about this life of Andrew's.

"It wasn't always like this," says Perdita once they are all seated and settled on the large verandah. "We started in a small apartment down there, in the barrios" she points to the ghetto area. The shambles of shacks on the far side of the city, now brightly painted with an air of defiance. "That wasn't always like that either. It was dirty. Smelled bad. But we survived and after all those years, now we are here."

While Perdita goes to the kitchen to organise refreshments Reg asks Gordon if he should mention the mine.

"I don't think, well maybe not today. I know we have to sometime; I don't want her to think that's why we are here."

"No?" says Reg. "Okay."

Teacups are laid out on the glass topped rattan table, with small side plates. "Royal Albert?" says Gordon. "We have these at home too."

"Yes, Papa sent these to me. He sent many things each month, just look around." Gordon begins to understand the FedEx receipts now as he sees Nova Scotia art on the walls, paintings by John Neville and Barbara McLean, Inuit artifacts he recognises from the Houston North Gallery in Lunenburg—sculptures in soapstone of seals and Inuit seal hunters adorning ornate highly polished credenzas. Out of place but looking absolutely at home.

There were never many works of art in the Drummond house in Indian Point. It was enough to have a fresh coat of paint every six or seven years. And that Gordon always did himself. In fact, he has no recollection of ever hiring anyone to do anything. And now here he is with a sister who hired drivers and cars and had valuable works of art in her house. Mixed emotions can be dangerous things, until now he has kept a steady nerve. Looked for the positive. He takes a gracious attitude as his mother always taught him.

His mind wanders back to Maryanne, his mother, but he stops himself wondering what she would have made of all of this.

"It's a beautiful spot," says Reg.

"We like it," says Perdita. "We feel we can breathe here. The city feels closed in, until you get to the water of course. Tomorrow, would you like to take a sail?"

Gordon is taken aback with the offer. He imagined this busy fifty-something capable woman would have things to do, a business to run maybe, a gold mine even, and yes, a court case hanging around her neck. "Aren't you busy?" he said.

"No, I've told everyone I am on holiday, vacation as you say, and as our father always said, 'it ain't goin' nowhere' is it?"

Gordon laughs, "He taught you some local Nova Scotia phrases then?"

"Oh yes, 'holy suff'rin' lightnin,' was always a favourite of his, I learned that by the time I was three years old. My mother was very cross."

"Your mother?" says Gordon." "Yes, Mama. She died."

"When was that? How long?" says Gordon.

"Oh twenty years," says Perdita. "After that Papa left."

"So what about a sail then, Gordie, you up for it?" says Reg, always adept at dealing with awkward situations.

"It's been a long time," says Gordon. "I think I can remember how to sail, bit like riding a bike isn't it?"

"You won't have to do anything," says Perdita, "just enjoy."

They drink their tea in silence, letting the jagged elements of the conversation permeate. Looking out to the horizon on the Pacific. Beginning to understand that life is not simple. That people can be more complex than they seem.

"So, tomorrow, the car will come at eight o'clock, bring you to the dock, we can spend all day away from everything. We can talk as much as you would like. I have questions, of course.

Eduardo will come with the food and drink. You need hats, sunscreen, long sleeves. Everything else will be there. The boat is called Drummond's Dream. You will like it I'm sure."

The car takes the three back to the apartment where Perdita says good evening and picks up her Mercedes convertible. "See you tomorrow, wear safe deck shoes, too," she calls as her car glides out through the iron gates and onto the cobble stones of the alley.

"Whirlwind," states Reg.

"You can say that again," says Gordon. "Is this all for real do you think?"

"We've got almost seven weeks to find out, I'd suggest we don't rush things. Let's enjoy the moments as they come."

"You're right," says Gordon. "But I can't help comparing. The modest life out on Indian Point—to all this." He opens his arms and points out through the French doors to the sky.

"I know," says Reg. "But this isn't you. And you don't know the story behind her at all, yet. Her mother for instance. The gold mine and all that. Dragging them from the ghetto to a high-class residential area. Setting up a grandson with training and then a restaurant. It all took money. Was it good money, Gordie? Do you really want to know the detail? And where does New York fit into the picture? Remember the passports?"

14.

Tuesday dawns golden and hopeful. By 7 am., Reg and Gordon have eaten a breakfast of fresh toasted bread with giant ripe peaches on the balcony. They have a backpack filled with sunscreen, bottles of water and spare shirts.

"It's a pity we didn't get to email home last night," says Gordon.

"Send a text on your phone," says Reg, "tell Joslyn you're running around like a blue- assed fly and will be back online tomorrow. Let's put tomorrow aside to catch up with some stuff I reckon."

"You're right," says Gordon, "I feel like I've had the wind punched out of me on the one hand, and some kind of exotic elixir pumped into me on the other. It really does feel like a dream. Oh look here, there's a message from Bill, he says he's coming down himself tomorrow with our other bags. When we get back from sailing, we should get that other bed made up. I'll email him back."

The car takes them to the Viña del Mar Yacht Club. The marina is resplendent in sail boats and ocean-going yachts of all sizes. Reg spots an orange West Wight Potter, "I used to have one like that," he says. "It was great fun, learned to sail in it. I called her The Saucy Sue, not officially, just my name for her." He waves to the young woman who is tinkering around on the small deck.

"Morning to you," he says.

She waves back. "Hi," she says, "Americano?"

"Canadian," calls Reg. "Top of the mornin' to ya!"

They follow the driver to the end of the marina where Perdita is standing on the dock.

She is wearing a navy and white striped cotton jersey with tight white pants and red deck shoes. She wears a red Roots Canadian Olympics ball cap and very large sunglasses.

"Good morning," she says. "All set?" She waves her hand towards the yacht. Reg estimates it is about forty feet. A sizeable cabin to the fore and three crew members busy with lines.

"Well, good morning to you, looks like we are all set. Nice boat. So this is Drummond's Dream," says Reg. "Is it yours?"

Perdita doesn't respond. Then, "I hope it still is," she says, "we may lose her in the case." "Case?" says Gordon, "the mine case?"

"Better not to talk about it now," says Perdita, "but we will, I may need your help. Do you know any good lawyers, these guys here are playing with me," she points towards the city.

"Funny you should say that..." begins Gordon. "What he means is..." says Reg.

"...Reg here is the very best there is, he's not just a good friend, he was Dad's lawyer and mine too."

"Is that why you have come?" says Perdita, her mouth becoming a hard gash in her face. "No, not at all," says Gordon, putting his arm around her shoulders, "Reg is a friend first and foremost. He came with me because, well because this is probably the scariest thing I have ever done. I have never travelled. And I have never flown before. Tell her Reg."

"All true, absolutely true," says Reg. "Friendship first. Law—as and when."

Perdita takes a visible deep breath. "Sorry, I have just been so screwed lately. Papa left a bit of a mess to clear up."

"I know the feeling," says Gordon.

They cast off from the dock and motor out of the marina. The city of Valparaiso looks like piles of quartz jumbled on a hillside, sparkling in the early morning sun. A glass of iced mango juice is put in Gordon's hand by Eduardo. "Can I call you Uncle Gordon?" he says.

"If you like," says Gordon, "I've never had a nephew before. Or you can just call me Gordie, that's what my friends call me."

The sit opposite each other on the deck, sipping juice and looking out to sea. "Mama doesn't do this often enough," he says, "she is too busy taking care of everything. Always business. Always on the computer. Or the phone. I'm so glad you are here. She may relax now. This has been a very long time to come."

Gordon smiles at the occasional lapse from perfect English. "I have tried to learn a little Spanish," he says, "especially for this visit."

"Bueno," says Eduardo, "you are a real Drummond."

"And this," he pats the seat beside him, "is Drummond's Dream." It is not a question. If the boat is about to be repossessed Gordon is already thinking about how he can get it up to Nova Scotia, to the Lunenburg Yacht Club. He plans to talk with Reg about it later. But for now, he is content to watch the coast of Chile, with its backdrop of mountains. The coast is rugged and stretches forever. Waves crash against the rocky shores. He understands from Reg's summaries of his research that Chile is almost all coast and mountains, stretching for two thousand miles, from Peru to Cape Horn. When he thinks of Cape Horn, he realises that transporting the yacht that route could be hazardous. Panama pops into his head. And with that the passport entries in his father's passport. What in the hell was he doing in Panama? The same as New York?

"Reg?" he says when Eduardo goes below to prepare midmorning snacks.

"Hmmm?" Reg is kicking back with his eyes closed, looking more relaxed than Gordon has ever seen him.

"Would it be possible to sail her home?"

"WHAT?" Reg sits up with a start. "This? Sail this home?"

"Yes, and shhhhh," says Gordon, "it's just a thought, better than letting her be repossessed."

"Repossessed?" says Reg. 'I'm wondering if you're possessed! Seriously though, we could talk to Bill tomorrow."

The afternoon dreams on. It reminds Gordon of an old Australian movie, Picnic at Hanging Rock. He once rented it from Blockbuster Videos in Bridgewater. The story haunted him. The faded colours and pan pipe music lingered in his mind long after. It was a story of Victorian schoolgirls at an Australian boarding school, one with strict discipline, the girls take a day's outing to a remote area, a beauty spot, for a picnic. Gordon remembers it was ages ago, his mother was still alive, and she wanted to watch it again before Gordie took it back to the store.

"It's supposed to be in by four, Ma," he'd said. "That's okay," she said, ' I'll pay the fine.

I just want to watch it once more."

Gordon absorbed the atmosphere of the movie and that's how this afternoon out on the yacht feels now. Everyone dozing after the excellent grilled fish lunch cooked by Eduardo.

They've drunk a chilled white Chilean wine with the fish and fresh salads, and afterwards Perdita pulls out an apple pie. "To make you think of home," she says, scooping ice-cream from the cooler, to top off the pie.

The crew quietly sail the yacht in a gentle southerly breeze about two miles off the shoreline. The movement of the boat and the occasional flip-flap of the sails lulling the four passengers into an afternoon sleep. Books slip off laps onto the deck, drinks stand on tables untouched, and no-one speaks.

Gordon surveys the scene as he wakes, aroused by a gull cawing overhead. He wonders if they are sailing into a black hole, like the one behind the hanging rock in Australia, never to be seen again. Always to remain a mystery. A mystery called Drummond's Dream.

But more gulls circle the boat, cawing and heeking and one by one, Reg, Perdita, and Eduardo wake, blink into the late afternoon sunshine, stretch, breathe deeply and murmur sounds that can only be good ones.

"Tea?" says Perdita.

"Coming right up," says Eduardo.

As Drummond's Dream motors into its berth in the Viña Del Mar Yacht Club, Reg and Gordon gather together their belongings.

"It's been so good," says Gordon, "thank you, Perdita." "Tomorrow?" she asks.

"Tomorrow we need to catch up on things," says Reg, hoping he is not interrupting or being too pushy. "But maybe by seven tomorrow evening we can get together. Bill Gladstone is coming out from Santiago."

"Gladstone?" she says, "Why?"

"He is bringing the rest of our luggage, we couldn't put it on the bus," says Gordon. "He's planning to stay for a couple of days, probably until the weekend. But if you need me, Reg can keep him entertained, I'm sure."

Perdita smiles. "Yes, I think I will need you. The case needs looking at. But first I'd like for you to come with me to the mine."

15

Perdita hands Gordon the file as they begin the long drive to the gold mining region. "It is a long way, bring a bag for overnight," she told him over supper the night before. Bill and Reg were silent as the Drummond siblings discussed the day ahead.

And now they swing out of the Valparaiso suburbs into open country and head towards the mountains. Gordon has little time to watch the scenery change from scrubland to breathtaking views as he reads the files.

It seems there is a Canadian connection. And it is through his father who still held a board position until his death. There is nothing to indicate that Gordon would step into his shoes.

Mining has stopped due to concerns over environmental issues and Perdita wants Gordon to see for himself. "Do you think Reg and Bill should come too?" he says before they finally climb into the limo.

" No," Perdita says. "Next time, but for now it should be the two of us."

It is early afternoon when they reach the Perdita Drummond Mine. Gordon has never seen such a blot on a landscape in all his days. "This is nothing on the Sydney Tar Ponds," he says quietly.

"What is Tar Ponds?"

"Oh, that was a huge environmental issue in Cape Breton, after the steel plants destroyed the land and the air around it, then closed down. Left something that appeared to be destroyed forever."

"And?"

"It's been addressed. Local people complained about ill health, cancer, many, many things. After all these years it has been transformed into a park."

"Could we look at such a solution?" says Perdita.

"No, but it is such a pity Reg can't see this, he might have a way out. Why is nobody working?"

"The government has suspended all working here until the case is resolved," she says, "we are losing money every day it is closed; we need that money to put forward a proposal and win the case. In other words, we have to build a case. A good one."

"Are they worried about the water supply?" says Gordon. "Yes," she says, "you seem knowledgeable about this."

"No, it's just that it crops up all over the world. I watch CNN. And PBS. All these cases have been resolved. You know the old saying?"

"What's that, Gordie?'

He smiles at her use of his name. "Money talks," he says.

"I've tried to tout for other investors," she says, "is that what you mean?"

"No, not at all," he says, "wait until we talk with Reg and Bill, You'll see what I mean. Reg has been involved in an ammolite mine in Alberta, he can show you the website with what they've done for the environment. The mines are shallow, just like this. Quite different to something like a coal mine, for instance."

Perdita takes Gordon on a tour of the mine. In the front office he dons protective garb and a hard hat. She gives him one that says 'A. Drummond.' "Yes," she says. "It was his." She pinches Gordon's cheeks; South American affection.

He looks at the photographs gracing the office walls. Photos of his dad cutting ribbons, smiling, surrounded by smiling Chilean miners. Gordon had no idea this was his father's former life. He tries to understand how he climbed from Cable Mechanic, as his occupation was described in the passport, to owning a gold mine. The tour takes them through an early part of the mine. Organised. Clean. A new experience for Gordon.

As they leave, he picks up a handful of gold dust from the ground. "May I?" he says. "Of course, it's your gold too," she says.

"You know, we have gold in Nova Scotia," he says. "Really?"

"Yes, the sort you go panning for, not mining. I often asked Dad if he wanted to give it a try, there is a place near us called Gold River, but he always said, 'I don't think so'."

They stay at a small bed and breakfast about five miles from the mine.

"Hola Maria," says Perdita, to the owner who comes from the kitchen wiping her hands on her yellow pinafore.

"Hola Madame," says Maria with a sad smile.

She shows them each to the small bedrooms telling them that food will be ready in half an hour.

"Good," says Perdita, "time for a shower. See you down there in thirty minutes, Gordie."

Gordon kicks off his shoes and lies back on the knitted blanket covering the bed. It reminds him of the blankets he has seen on the Antiques Road Show and guesses this is an example of local Indian work. He would like to find something like this to take back for Pea. Maybe one for Louie, too. Yes, two blankets. He will ask Perdita on the drive back.

He doesn't shower, but drifts into a dreamy sleep. He wakes to find Perdita banging on his door. "Come on," she says, "the food will be cold."

They eat in a familiar silence now. So much has happened in such a short time. Gordon's mind is on fire with thoughts, problems, solutions. He smiles, reminding himself that he thought he was to face a boring retirement with no friends and nothing to do.

Now he has so many friends, family, and so much to do he doesn't know what to tackle first.

"Can I buy some of those nice blankets to take back?" he says, as they drink their strong coffee, watching the sun set over the mountains. "What, the local blankets?" she says.

"Yes, don't laugh, but I think my little dog might like one. I was going to ask on our drive back, but…"

She does laugh, but not unkindly. "I will take you," she says, "before you leave for Canada, I will take you. You can choose and they will ship for you. Don't let me forget. With all these other things, I have much on my mind."

16.

Bill and Reg have a fruitful day with Gordon gone. After talking through the possible ways to get Drummond's Dream up to Nova Scotia, Reg fills Bill in on the gold mine case. "Yes, I do know all about the case, I've been watching it carefully. It's the same all over the world. The local Indians have made some really good points. This could be a perfect example of a solution for these environmental issues to the world."

"What are you saying, Bill, the solution could be a profitable business too?" "You've got it, you and I think along the same lines, Reg."

"But the wheel is already invented," says Reg. "Take Alberta." "Oil?" says Bill.

"No," says Reg. "Ammolite."

"Never heard of it," says Bill, "can you tell me more?"

Reg explains how ammolite is a unique gem accessed through shallow mining procedures. How after each kilometre of land is carefully scraped and dug back to reveal the strata of ammolite, the landscaping begins and the land is not just restored to what it once was, but with planting of trees and shrubs, it is being transformed into a beauty spot. A place for nature to take forward and become something it never was before. "The government will use it as an example for future projects, I guess," he says.

"Interesting," says Bill. "Here, let me show you."

Reg logs onto the internet and finds the website for the ammolite mine. There are photos and video clips of the before and after. Bill is impressed and says so.

"You know, you two guys were destined to come down here," he says, "you are bringing ideas and knowledge that not just Gordon's family, but the industry as a whole needs."

They open a couple of bottles of beer and sit on the verandah and talk about more personal things, "Are you married?" says Reg.

"Nope. You?"

"No, not now, I was for a short time when I was young. Didn't work out." "Gordon?"

"No, him neither. Looked after his mother. Then his father. Devoted his life to them. When his dad died, Gordie thought it was all over. He had nothing to look forward to. I'm the only real friend he's got. It helps that I'm his lawyer too." Reg laughs.

Bill laughs too. "Amazing what death can do," he says. "But this is a bit extreme. A father living a double life, two families, hidden assets and all that."

"It's been an emotional eye-opener for Gordie. In my job I turn up family secrets, but never anything like this," says Reg.

"Happened to me a couple of times too," says Bill, "but as you say, nothing like this.

What time did you say they'll be back?"

"Not 'til after dark, fancy going out for something to eat?"

When Gordon arrives home, Perdita comes in with him,

"Just for a few moments," she says, "I really do need to get back too."

Reg and Bill are back from the restaurant and are sitting at the dining table which is covered in paper, note pads, and the laptop is open, whirring away.

"Hey you two," says Reg, beaming.

"Hey?" says Gordon, not expecting such a welcome. "Hi," says Perdita, "you must be Bill."

"Yes, sorry, how rude of me," Bill stands and shakes hands with Perdita. "We've never met, but I've heard so much about you."

She looks at Gordon and Reg.

"No, not through these two," he adds, "but you are well known in the business world. All good," he adds.

Over the course of two weeks, Reg, Gordon, Bill and Perdita meet to talk through the problems and solution options. Perdita wants to get Drummond's Dream out of the picture—she knows it could be the first thing to be seized by authorities. She transfers ownership to Reg who gets onto a guy he knows in Ottawa, an offshore qualified skipper. He can fly down with a small crew and sail it up the west coast of South America to the Panama Canal. Cross through the Canal and sail through the Caribbean Sea to Florida. From there they'll sail the inter coastal waterway into the North Atlantic, up the New England States coast, across the Gulf of Maine and then up the southwest coast of Nova Scotia to Lunenburg. "He thinks it would take about three months," Reg tells Bill.

The four settle for that and then get down to looking at how to handle the gold mine issues.

Gordon feels very much that Reg is in his element. Bill Gladstone and Reg work in tandem for hours, pouring over project proposals until it's agreed that they'll bring a consultant down from Alberta Ammolite. His name is Joel Zwicker, and they go into Santiago to meet him at the airport the following Thursday.

The apartment in Valparaiso is getting crowded. The owner, Jock, pops in one afternoon to ask if they'd like the one next door too as the booking for that has just been cancelled. Gordon snaps it up. That's where they put Joel.

"S'great this," says Joel. "The dining room is bigger in this one too, would it make a better meeting room?" This is Joel's first solution to a problem; solved before it became one.

By the court date, Reg and Gordon have been in Chile for three and a half weeks. It feels like forever. Bill trips back and forth to Santiago to keep his law business in check, but he has a good and loyal partner and much of their work is done on the phone or via the internet giving Bill all the flexibility he could wish for. He has explained that winning this case could be a real coup for the partnership and set them apart from the competition. With Joel Zwicker, descended from Canadian aborigines, as their expert witness, Bill is confident that the case is in the bag.

Meanwhile Gordon and Perdita deal with family concerns. Getting to know each other. Talking about the past. Trying to regret nothing but finding it difficult.

"What about your mother?" asks Gordon one day. "She loved him," is her simple reply.

"He must have loved her too," says Gordon. "Yes, very much. They did marry you know." "But how?"

"I know, now I think it probably wasn't legal, they married in the church. Come, I'll show you."

She takes him to the Iglesia Anglicana, St. Paul's Church. It turns out to be the small church where the bus dropped them on their first day. In a way, it looks like an upturned boat, with no tower and no cross. It seems that it was built by English settlers and is now a national monument.

"Not Roman Catholic then?'

"No," says Perdita, "Mama was catholic, but Papa was not. Lutheran, he said, so this was a good solution. This area was part of the old British community, this church was built by a famous architect, Lloyd or a name like that."

"William Lloyd," says Gordon, touching a plaque by the door.

Together they admire the stained-glass windows and the paintings of the Ten Commandments on either side of the altar. Perdita points to 'thou shalt not commit adultery', and laughs. Her voice rings through the tiny church and Gordon feels a happiness he has not felt for many years. It is as close to euphoria as he can imagine.

"She is buried out here."

They walk through the churchyard among the graves with English names. William Thomson, Grace Henderson, Amelia Wright. And they stop at Maria Anna Drummond. There are fresh flowers. The grave is trimmed, the stone bright white and scrubbed.

"I come every week," she says. "You'll do the same for Papa, won't you?"

"I will, that's a promise, I'll send you photos. Right now it is high in snow, I talked with Joslyn last night. They've had a big storm."

"So cold," says Perdita, "to be lying in the ground, so cold like that." She shivers, then says, "Joslyn, who is she?"

"A work colleague," says Gordon, "she is taking care of my little dog for me. I miss her." "Joslyn?"

"No, my dog, Pea—well, Jos too I suppose. She is just a friend. I have no girlfriend." "Reg?"

"He has no girlfriend either."

"No," she laughs, 'I thought maybe you and Reg..."

Gordon laughs too. "No, we are not gay," he says, "two guys can be friends, can't we?" "Of course, but I do not want you to be lonely, back in the cold north, I have seen what it

is like. No colour, bare, white, dark."

"You will come in the summer?" says Gordon. "You can stay at Drummond, that's our house. We can sail the Atlantic. I will learn to cook pancakes and serve them with maple syrup. Bring Eduardo. I will show you the other side of life."

"You have said it all," says Perdita. "The other side of life. It is true all life has another side, and we will only find it if we look. It took courage for you to come."

"As it did for you to come up for the funeral. How did you know? I've never really worked that one out."

"He wrote," she says. "Sent with FedEx. A note and the keys to the trunk. He knew." "Are you saying he knew he was dying?"

"Yes, he wrote something like 'I have reached the end now my Perdie, that's what he called me, I've reached my end. It has been good. Let there be no more lies.' I watched the internet for signs of a death announcement and as soon as I saw, I booked my ticket. I stayed in Halifax for four days afterwards trying to find some way to contact you. But I didn't have your braveness."

"I have something else to tell you," he says. "Yes?"

"My mother was also Maryanne." Perdita is silent.

"Coincidence? Maybe. Maybe that's all it is. There is just one more question," says Gordon, "then we can leave the past behind and move on."

"Yes?"

"Isn't there a husband? You? Are you married? You use the Drummond name."

"I never changed my name when I married," she says. "Papa said it would complicate the mine's paperwork. Then my husband died. Eduardo was just a tiny boy. There was an explosion. At the mine. It is not a happy place for me. He is not buried anywhere. Unless you count the mine."

Gordon takes his sister's hands in his. "We were both in very difficult situation," he says. "I was already in shock; I didn't have the warning you did. In the end this has turned out better, I think. I have been able to take a look at my father's life without anyone getting hurt. When you come, we will do some of the things he did in the past twenty years in Nova Scotia. Quite different from here that's for sure. Now come back to the apartment, we'll make tea and find out how the guys are getting on."

17.

The initial hearing takes place in Santiago and the team, as that is how they now refer to themselves, check into the Radisson Plaza.

"Welcome back, how many rooms?"

"We are five, so we will take what you can offer, all together please," says Bill, "I could just go home," he says to Reg and Joel, "but I think it's best we stay secreted here, don't you?"

"Good plan," says Joel, "it's quite a country, I do hope I get chance for a bit of sight- seeing. The trip to the mine sure opened my eyes as to the place's versatility."

"If all goes well, we'll make sure you get the royal treatment," says Reg.

The Radisson gives them four suites on the top floor. "All for yourselves," the desk clerk says, "no-one to bother you. You are here for the case, yes?"

"How news travels," Perdita says in Spanish, "Si," she says to the desk clerk. "Here for the case."

"Good luck then," he says, "I hope all is good for you."

They sit around the large table in the bridal suite until 2 am., then Gordon says, "We should call it a night. We must be there for ten, right?"

"Yes," says Bill. "We are ready, well, as ready as we'll ever be. I'll arrange for room service breakfast for us all here at

103

seven and we can go through everything one last time."

The court hearing is almost a non-event. The court room is not as packed as Gordon expects. He feels that somehow the information they were to present had leaked and found to be favourable. Joel speaks well as an expert witness. He shows photographs of the ammolite mine in Alberta; the beautiful park land with colourful birds in the trees and butterflies perched on large pink echinacea flowers. He is asked about timeframes and the water run offs and costs. There is no need for an interpreter either. The English spoken in the court room is impeccable. By 1 pm the hearing is over. Their proposal has met with approval. The panel asks for a project plan to be presented within ninety days. The sooner they have it, the sooner the mine can reopen.

"You may need to stay on," Perdita says to Joel.

"Not a problem," he says with a grin. "Can't wait to draw up the plans."

Reg and Gordon are in their final week in Valparaiso. Perdita is taking them to the weaving co- operative in Indian country. Reg doesn't question why but has a good idea that this is something to do with Pea. He hasn't ceased to be amazed that Gordon and Joslyn have spoken on Skype most evenings. Chile is just an hour ahead of Nova Scotia, so after supper for Reg and Gordon, is before supper for Jos.

Reg has watched as Gordon talked to Pea, telling her he will be home soon, and something makes him wonder if he should think about getting a dog, too.

"We could go for walks together. All of us, Jos with

Louie, and you and Pea, and me with mine," says Reg. "I like the look of Louie; how do I go about adopting a retired racing dog like that?"

Gordon explains to him about GPAC, Greyhound Pets of Atlantic Canada, a volunteer organization that brings up retired racers from the tracks in Florida. "You should see them when they arrive," says Gordon. "All colours and sizes, all eager to have a happy retirement. You couldn't do much better than a greyhound."

"Are they old?" says Reg.

"No, not at all, although you could apply for a senior, Louie wasn't even two when Jos took him, he just wasn't a very good racer, that's all."

The two men begin to think about going home, about the journey ahead of them, not just physically, but the emotions involved too.

Reg and Bill have become firm friends. Arrangements for visits are talked through. Reg even looks into buying an apartment in the same complex as the one they were using. "Jock is the manager, he has the keys and lets people in and out etc.," says Reg. "You just block out the weeks you want to use it yourself and the rest of the time people pay rent, just like we have, and it helps to pay for it. Bill can get someone to take care of the conveyancing for me. What do you think?"

"I think you should sleep on it, in fact I think you should wait until you get home before making a final decision," says Gordon, "maybe we're all carried away with the sunshine and mangoes."

"Not like you," says Reg, "I thought you'd be all for it, in the circumstances."

"Well, I am, of course I am. I can't wait to get home now, but then I'll be looking forward to coming back, and you're right, for such a long visit, the accommodation has been the biggest cost."

"It's alright for you, you have family now you can stay with."

Gordon knows Reg is kidding, "I'd rather stay independently," he says, "tell you what, why don't we buy one between us."

18.

Air Canada flight AC093 takes off on time for Toronto. After a flight that seems to go on forever, they touch down and find they have four hours to kick around Pearson Airport.

At Tim Hortons they order a snack pack of chocolate glazed Timbits and two double doubles and watch humanity pass before them. But Gordon doesn't see them, already he is looking forward to home. To the wood stove in the kitchen, to seeing just what mail has piled up. And to Pea. He wants to hold her tight and tell her he will never leave her again, and of that he is quite sure now. Next time, she will go too.

He went to Chile in search of his father's past and found a family. He found a smart, vibrant sister who has business troubles as well as personal ones, and a fatherless nephew who has promised to visit in just three months' time.

"Bit of a roller coaster ride, ain't it?" says Reg, nodding at the people jostling by, pulling suitcases on wheels, adjusting backpacks, clutching papers, answering cell phone calls. "Not my idea of fun really. But hey, we had a good time, didn't we?"

Gordon looks at him, "We did indeed. We turned something that could have been a disaster into a trip of a lifetime. And if you ever find that your father led a double life, make sure the other was somewhere warm and sunny, Australia maybe, then I'll come with you to dig up the dirt."

"Old Murray? I don't think he ever left The Bay," says

Reg, "well not to my knowledge anyway."

"Just look at what I didn't know," says Gordon, "I had no idea, no idea at all…"

"So what about New York then?" says Reg,

"New York? Dad? No, I thought we'd leave the rest of his story stay right where it is. Let sleeping dogs lie, so to speak. But Perdita and I talked last night, she wants to dig a little deeper."

The 5 am. flight to Halifax is called. Reg and Gordon board for the final leg of their journey home.

As they land at Stanfield International and taxi to the terminal, Gordon looks at the land. His homeland. And notices the birch buds just starting to leaf out into a delicate lime green haze. Announcing a new spring. He knows that the pussy willows will be sporting their silken buds on the bank beside the house, his home. Drummond.

And there'll be masses of white, purple and yellow crocuses opening on his parents' grave.

Perdita

I waved my big brother, Gordon, and his good friend, Reg, off in departures. It was a sad day for us all, "I had no idea I would feel like this," Gordon said. Dabbing his eyes with a large white handkerchief. I'd given him a set of fine linen handkerchiefs after I found him using rough paper towels or Kleenex.

"You deserve better," I'd said the night I gave them to him. He pulled one out and admired the blue embroidered 'G' in the corner. "So much makes sense now," he said, "and yet…"

"Yes?" I said.

"So much doesn't. We're not finished are we?"

"Nowhere near," I said. "I'll be up in the summer, and we can pick up the threads of where we've left off, but for now, I am so very happy that you found me."

"And I you," he said.

"Don't worry," said Reg, "I'll keep my eye on him."

I watched the two elderly men work their way through security, smiling, being courteous, joking with officials. Turning for that final wave to me. No excess baggage either, I'd managed to convince them that shipping would be so much easier for them; for the hand-woven blankets and local pottery to arrive on the doorstep at the Drummond house without them having to lift a finger. I hoped Jos would appreciate the gifts and will see that she, not just his little dog, is never far from Gordon's thoughts.

I didn't drive straight home. I needed time to assimilate all that had happened. How this very traditional man demonstrated his love for family. A family he didn't know existed. Instead of being accusatory and thinking bad of his father, my mother, me and my family, he embraced us and I was able to see how Papa's good genes had blessed us both.

Epilogue

2021

In spite of Covid restrictions, I'm here with Gordon now for another summer. I've been every year since Gordon's first visit five years ago.

We've taken Drummond's Dream out to the islands a few times. It has made me understand so much more about the extreme contrast of my father's life.

And we've talked. Jos comes too, she and Gordon are now what young people call, an item. I knew it would happen. And nothing to do with dog fleas at all. We joke about that. Very sadly, Gordon's little dog Pea died last year. I know he misses her all the time. He talks of her a lot and tells me more about how our father called her Perdy.

With the power of the internet, Eduardo (my son) and Jos, found out what our father did in New York all those Christmases years back. And it was nothing to do with other women as we were beginning to think, but for respite. It turned out our father had an aversion to Christmas festivities and found a silent retreat just outside New York where he could recharge before returning to the double life he led. I suspect the increasing challenges with the mine didn't help.

As a young man, he'd arrived in Chile as a cable mechanic. At the end of his business career he owned the mine. Juggling his family life must have added to the stress.

And while he never spoke of his other Canadian family

to me. Nor vice versa to Gordon, he left the trail open for Gordon and me to find one another.

- end -

Acknowledgements

I must firstly give thanks for the ten years I had with Tilly (Hollowell Chantilly Lace 2012 - 2022), my much loved beautiful white and black whippet girl who lives on through Pea in this story. And by association, Alex and Diane for bringing her into my life.

Also Pierre and Rose who knew exactly how to sail a yacht from Chile to Nova Scotia; it was do-able after all. And by association, GPAC (Greyhound Pets of Atlantic Canada).

To Dennis, whose pop-up antiques in Liverpool and the old cardboard box which held (at the bottom under piles of old photos) the dusty passports that gave birth to the story idea. And to the 3-day novel project (2013) in which the first draft happened.

Thank you to my loyal and oh-so-honest alpha and beta readers: Kat, Elke, Vicki, Marg, Pam (RR), Pam (S), Kimberly, J.P. Vincent, Bruce, Debbie, and John. Your eagle eyes are remarkable. Not forgetting the really early readers, Richard and Jan. And the most recent readers, Adam and Laura. Forever grateful.

To my flag-waver-in-chief, Vicki, for the hours, nay—days, weeks, and months when you've been there for me, FaceTiming on Sunday afternoons, extinguishing my doubts, cheering me on, and making me laugh. Non-stop showerings of love for you and for Jim for texting laughter at times when laughter is always the best medicine.

None of my books would exist without Arne. Thank you are words too small for your immense support, encouragement, astuteness and love. And for dragging me off down the coast for fish and chips (to the very eatery in this story) when you knew I just needed a break.

To Summer Stewart for saying 'yes' again. And thanks always to all the team at Unsolicited Press for turning my manuscripts into books. For making them real. And for making the entire book creation process an absolute joy.

And finally, thank you always to this peaceful corner of the world, where thinking, observing, dreaming and creating can happen. You just have to give it a chance.

Nova Scotia, Spring 2023

About the Author

S.B. Borgersen is a British/Canadian author, of middle England and Hebridean ancestry, whose favoured genres are flash and micro fiction, novellas, and poetry.

Her books, Fishermen's Fingers, While the Kettle Boils, Of Daisies and Dead Violins, Eva Matson, and The Sequence Dance, are published by Unsolicited Press.

Since 2000 Sue's writing has won prizes, been mentioned in Hansard and published internationally in literary journals and anthologies. The list of publications is extensive and can be found at www.sueborgersen.com

She is a member of The Society of Authors, The Writers' Federation of Nova Scotia, and Genre Writers of Atlantic Canada.

Sue writes from her home on Nova Scotia's south shore where she lives with her patient husband and two lovable but rowdy dogs.

S.B. Borgersen writes every day.

About the Press

Unsolicited Press is based out of Portland, Oregon and focuses on the works of the unsung and underrepresented. As a womxn-owned, all-volunteer small publisher that doesn't worry about profits as much as championing exceptional literature, we have the privilege of partnering with authors skirting the fringes of the lit world. We've worked with emerging and award-winning authors such as Shann Ray, Amy Shimshon-Santo, Brook Bhagat, Kris Amos, and John W. Bateman.

Learn more at unsolicitedpress.com. Find us on twitter and instagram.

www.ingramcontent.com/pod-product-compliance
Lightning Source LLC
Chambersburg PA
CBHW061548310726
48972CB00008B/2667